The Forging of a Samurai

Daughter of Blood: Hinadori Book II
Juro Go

LPS Publishing House LLC

Prologue

The scent of spices and overripe fruit wafted up from Tuchi Market, mingling with the crisp night air as Hinadori found himself standing on the familiar bridge. Moonlight glinted off the river's surface, casting everything in an ethereal glow. It was here, on this very spot, that his life had changed forever.

"Hinadori," a voice cut through the night, sharp as a blade, one he'd recognize anywhere.

He turned to see Noke approaching, her steps as silent as ever. She looked different somehow... stronger, more assured. The hard edges of street life had been honed to a deadly precision, her movements exuding a quiet but unmistakable power. Or purpose?

"Noke," he breathed, a mix of emotions swirling in his chest. "I didn't think I'd see you again so soon."

She offered a half-smile, leaning against the bridge railing. "Soon? Hell, it feels like a lifetime since I saw you last."

Hinadori nodded, realizing the truth of her words. How long had it been since that life-altering moment when he chose to follow Saito through the gates of the Bushido Academy? Days blurred together in a haze of training and trials.

"I suppose you're right," he conceded. "So much has happened. Sometimes I can hardly believe we're the same street rats who used to scrounge for scraps in the market."

Noke's eyes gleamed with a hint of mischief. "Speak for yourself. I was always destined for greatness."

"Do you remember," Hinadori began, his voice growing wistful, "those dinners with Akari? How she always managed to scrape together extra food, no matter how tight things were?"

Noke scoffed. "Yeah, yeah. First time I didn't have to fight for every scrap. What's your point?"

Hinadori nodded, a lump forming in his throat. "Just thinking about how far we've come, I guess."

There was silence. Hinadori looked at his feet.

He was surprised when Noke let out a sharp laugh.

"Remember that time you tried to impress her with your 'special' rice balls?" Noke chuckled, nudging him with her elbow.

Hinadori groaned, covering his face in mock embarrassment. "Don't remind me. I thought adding those berries was so clever."

"Until we all turned purple for a day," Noke finished, shaking her head. "But Akari... she just smiled and ate every last one."

They fell into a comfortable silence, both lost in the bittersweet memories of those shared meals. Akari had been more than just a caretaker; she'd been the closest thing to family either of them had known in a long time.

"I miss those nights," Hinadori admitted softly. "The warmth, the laughter. Everything seemed simpler then."

Noke's expression grew serious. "We can't go back, Hinadori. But we can make sure Akari's sacrifice wasn't for nothing. We survive. We get stronger. That's how we honor her."

They fell into a comfortable silence, gazing out over the sleeping city. Memories flooded Hinadori's mind – late nights huddled together for warmth, sharing meager meals, watching each other's backs. Noke had been more than just a friend; she'd been family when he had none.

"I miss this sometimes," he admitted softly. "The simplicity of it all. Survival was hard, but at least I knew where I stood."

Noke turned to face him, her expression serious. "Do you regret it? Leaving?"

"I don't regret it," he said firmly. "The Academy is brutal, but I'm becoming stronger every day. I'm going to make a difference, Noke. I can feel it." He paused and then repeated it again, "I don't regret it. No. But, I do wonder... What if I had stayed? What if I had gone with you instead?"

"You can't live in 'what ifs,' Hinadori," Noke chided gently. "We each chose our own path. The real question is: are you happy with yours?"

The weight of her words settled over him. The lack of remorse was one thing. But happiness was another question.

Was he happy?

The Bushido Academy had pushed him to his limits, broken him down and rebuilt him. There were days when every muscle ached, when his spirit felt crushed beneath the relentless demands of his training. But there were also moments of triumph, of skills honed to razor sharpness, of a growing sense of purpose that filled a void he hadn't even known existed.

"I think... I think I am," he said slowly. "It's not easy, but I feel like I'm becoming someone I can be proud of. Someone who can make a difference."

Noke nodded approvingly. "Good. That's all that matters in the end."

"What about you?" Hinadori asked, curious. "How has your journey been?"

A shadow passed over Noke's face, gone so quickly he almost thought he'd imagined it. "Different," she said simply. "But necessary. I'm learning things about myself... about the world... that I never could have imagined."

Hinadori sensed there was more she wasn't saying, but he didn't push. They had both chosen paths that led to secrets and hidden knowledge. Some things, perhaps, were better left unshared.

"I worry about you sometimes," he confessed. "The Shugendo ways... they're not always kind."

Noke's laugh was sharp. "And you think the Bushido Academy is a walk in the cherry blossoms? We've both chosen difficult roads, Hinadori. But they're the ones we need to walk."

He couldn't argue with that. Still, a part of him ached at the distance growing between them – not just physical, but in experience and understanding.

"Do you ever think about that night?" he asked suddenly. "When we saw the Wind of Death?"

Noke's entire demeanor changed at the mention of the legendary sword. Her eyes blazed with an intensity that almost made Hinadori take a step back.

"Every day," she whispered. "I can still feel it calling to me, even now."

Hinadori suppressed a shudder. He remembered all too well the otherworldly pull of that blade, the way it seemed to sing with barely contained power. But where it had filled him with a mix of awe and terror, Noke had been transfixed, as if the sword spoke to something deep within her very soul.

"Be careful, Noke," he warned. "There are forces at work here that we don't fully understand."

She turned to him, a fierce determination etched into every line of her face. "That's exactly why I have to do this, Hinadori. Someone needs to understand. Someone needs to be strong enough to wield that power, to make sure it doesn't fall into the wrong hands."

"And you think that someone is you?"

"I know it is," she said with unwavering conviction.

Hinadori wanted to argue, to tell her she was being reckless, but he bit his tongue.

Who was he to judge?

Hadn't he thrown himself headlong into a world of strict discipline and martial prowess, all on the word of a mysterious samurai?

"Just... promise me you'll be careful," he said instead. "And remember, no matter what happens, you're not alone. If you ever need me—"

"I know," Noke cut him off, but her tone was gentle. "The same goes for you, you know. We may have chosen different paths, but we'll always be connected."

As if to emphasize her point, she reached out and clasped his hand. The warmth of her touch seemed to spread through him, chasing away the chill of the night.

"I should go," she said reluctantly. "And you... you have challenges ahead of you that will require all your strength."

Hinadori nodded, knowing she was right but not wanting the moment to end. "Will I see you again?"

Noke's smile was enigmatic. "Count on it. Our stories are far from over, Hinadori. In fact, I think they're only just beginning."

With that, she turned and began to walk away. Hinadori watched her go, feeling a mix of sadness and anticipation. As her figure faded into the mist that had begun to gather at the far end of the bridge, he called out one last time.

"Noke!"

She paused, looking back over her shoulder.

"Thank you," he said simply. "For everything."

She nodded once, and then she was gone.

...

The dream began to dissolve around him, the solid planks of the bridge turning insubstantial beneath his feet. As reality reasserted itself, Hinadori clung to the memory of Noke's words, of the warmth of her hand in his.

His eyes snapped open, and for a moment, disorientation washed over him. Gone was the familiar sight of Tuchi Market, the comforting presence of his oldest friend. Instead, bare walls greeted him, the room sparse and unfamiliar. Every inch of his body ached, a testament to the brutal training he'd endured.

Hinadori struggled to sit up, wincing as pain lanced through his ribs. A spasm of pain shot through his body as the events of the past weeks came back to him – the relentless drills, the harsh discipline, the constant push to break him down and rebuild him as a true warrior of the Bushido Academy. He was being forged into a Samurai, and the process was far from gentle.

He glanced around the small, isolated room. This was his consequence for...

For what?

The memories were hazy, clouded by exhaustion and the lingering tendrils of his dream. He remembered a fight, a flash of pain, a moment of blind rage that had overtaken him.

And then... *nothing.*

How had he ended up here?

More importantly, how was he going to prove himself worthy of the path he'd chosen?

With a groan, Hinadori forced himself to his feet. His legs trembled, threatening to give out beneath him. But he gritted his teeth and remained standing. He was no longer the street rat of Tuchi Market, scraping by on luck and quick wits. He had chosen this life, had promised himself he would become someone worthy of wielding a blade in defense of others.

Whatever trials lay ahead, he would face them. For himself, for the memory of Omo, and yes, even for Noke... though their paths had diverged, he knew their destinies were somehow intertwined.

Hinadori attempted to take a deep breath, but his ribs screamed in protest, threatening to crack under the strain. Centering himself, as he had been taught, became a battle against his own battered body. The dream of Noke lingered in his mind, a bittersweet reminder of all he'd left behind. For a moment, he considered trying to send her a message, to reach out across the distance that separated them.

His hand moved towards the small writing desk in the corner of the room, but he stopped himself. No. This was his journey now. He had to walk it alone, at least for the time being.

With a mixture of regret and resolve, Hinadori turned away from the desk. Whatever lay ahead, he would face it head-on. The true test was only beginning.

Chapter 1- Where Legends Breathe

The iron-wrought gates of the Bushido Academy loomed before Hinadori like the maw of some ancient beast, ready to swallow him whole.

He stood rooted to the spot, his heart doing a frantic taiko drum solo in his chest. The weight of his choice - leaving Noke and the familiar squalor of Tuchi Market behind - sat heavy as a sumo wrestler on his shoulders.

"Having second thoughts, street rat?"

Saito's gruff voice cut through his spiraling thoughts like a hot knife through tofu.

Hinadori whirled to face the samurai who'd dragged him on this mad journey. Saito's face was a mask of stone, his eyes chips of obsidian. Any hint of the gruff-but-occasionally-kind reluctant guide had evaporated like morning dew, replaced by something harder, colder.

Squaring his shoulders, Hinadori met that unyielding gaze. "Not a chance."

A ghost of a smirk flitted across Saito's face, there and gone faster than a pickpocket's fingers. "We'll see about that."

Hinadori followed Saito deeper into the Academy grounds, the looming structures growing more imposing with each step. Hinadori got his first eyeful of the world beyond - and felt his jaw hit the dirt.

The Bushido Academy sprawled before him like something out of a fever dream. Where the Shugendo temple had been all warm earth tones and natural beauty, this place was a study in stark contrasts and barely contained power. Pale stone buildings with swooping rooflines stood proud as peacocks against the backdrop of mist-shrouded mountains. Meticulously manicured gardens gave way to training grounds where figures moved in deadly dances that made Hinadori's street brawls look like drunken flailing.

But it was the central keep that truly snagged Hinadori's attention and refused to let go. It thrust up from the heart of the Academy like a blade aimed at the heavens, its many levels disappearing into the swirling mist. At its peak, barely visible through the soup-thick air, sat a structure that seemed to glow with an otherworldly light.

"Is that The Chamber?" Hinadori asked, remembering rumors he heard years ago. "Home to the masters who pull the Academy's strings?"

Saito did not respond.

A shiver tap-danced its way down Hinadori's spine. "Who are they? These masters?"

Saito's face darkened like storm clouds gathering.

"The Chamber," Saito said, his voice tight. "You will be called to meet them and state your purpose. Be prepared, be ready."

Those words hung in the air like the stench of week-old fish as they began their climb into the Academy proper. The stone stairs seemed to go on forever, each step feeling like scaling a mountain. Hinadori's legs screamed in protest, his recent wound throbbing like an angry hornet's nest. But he gritted his teeth and pushed on, determined not to show even a whisper of weakness.

As they ascended, Hinadori became acutely aware of eyes boring into him from all sides. Figures lurked in windows and on balconies, their faces hidden but their judgment palpable. He felt like a cricket tossed into a pit of hungry lizards - exposed, vulnerable, woefully out of his depth.

"They're watching," he muttered to Saito, trying to keep the tremor out of his voice.

The samurai didn't miss a beat. "They're always watching. Every breath you take here is a test, boy. Tattoo that on the inside of your eyelids."

They weaved through a maze of courtyards, each more impressive than the last. In one, a group of students moved through sword forms with the fluid grace of water over smooth stones. In another, archers loosed arrows at targets so far away Hinadori could barely make them out through the mist. The display of skill made his street-honed abilities feel about as useful as a paper umbrella in a typhoon.

"This is where you'll start your journey," Saito said, gesturing to a stark building that looked about as welcoming as a hungry tiger. "The Hall of First Steps. Every student, no matter if they're the Emperor's own brat or gutter trash like you, starts here."

As they approached, Hinadori's eyes locked onto faded rust-colored stains marring the stone steps. His stomach did a backflip. "What happened there?"

Saito's voice could have frozen sake. "Failure."

Before Hinadori could wrap his brain around the implications of that single, terrifying word, a commotion erupted nearby. A crowd had gathered, their attention laser-focused on two figures squaring off in a training ring.

"Well, well," Saito said, a hint of interest creeping into his voice. "Looks like we've stumbled into a show. Pay attention, boy. This is the kind of skill you'll need to not end up as a bloodstain on those steps."

Hinadori watched, transfixed, as the two combatants circled each other like wary wolves. Both were older than him, their bodies honed to lethal perfection. One, a towering young man with hair as wild as a tanuki's fur, wielded a katana that gleamed like bottled starlight. The other, a lithe woman with eyes sharp enough to cut, danced with a pair of wickedly curved daggers.

For a heartbeat, the world held its breath. Then, in a blur that made Hinadori's eyes water, they clashed. Steel sang against steel, the sound ringing out like a demonic bell. The swordsman's blade was poetry in motion, but the woman was smoke given form, twisting and weaving through his attacks like they were moving in slow motion.

Hinadori realized he'd stopped breathing, mesmerized by the deadly ballet unfolding before him. This was nothing like the brutal, graceless brawls he'd been part of on the streets. This was art and death tangled up in a lover's embrace.

The fight reached its crescendo in the blink of an eye. The swordsman overextended on a thrust, and in that fraction of a heartbeat, the woman struck. One dagger trapped his blade while the other kissed his throat, drawing a thin line of crimson.

"Yield," the woman's voice carried the finality of a coffin lid slamming shut.

The swordsman's face twisted like he'd bitten into a rotten plum, but he nodded. "I yield."

The gathered students erupted in a cacophony of cheers and curses, many exchanging what looked suspiciously like betting tokens.

"Not bad," Saito muttered, though whether he was talking to Hinadori or himself was anybody's guess. "Kagemi's gotten sharper. The Chamber will be pleased."

Hinadori's mind was a whirlwind of questions, each fighting to be the first one out of his mouth. Who were these incredible warriors? How long before he could move like that? And what in the name of all the kami was this Chamber that seemed to loom over everything like a hungry ghost?

As if plucking the thoughts straight from Hinadori's head, Saito clapped a hand on his shoulder. The touch was about as comforting as a snake coiling around his neck. "The road ahead is long and full of pitfalls, boy. Many walk through these gates. Few survive the trials, and only the elite emerge as true Samurai. The weak are broken and discarded."

Hinadori clenched his fists, meeting Saito's gaze with all the fire he could muster. "Bring it on. I'm ready for whatever this place can throw at me."

A smile as cold as midwinter frost played at the corners of Saito's mouth. "We'll see about that."

They pressed on, weaving through the Academy's labyrinthine pathways. With each step, Hinadori felt the air grow thicker, charged with an energy that made the hairs on the back of his neck stand at attention.

As they neared the base of the central keep, its shadow fell over them like a physical weight. Hinadori craned his neck, trying to see the top, but it was lost in the roiling mist.

"This is where we part ways," Saito said abruptly. "From here, you'll be assigned to your *kūkan* and start your training. Remember, boy – trust is a luxury you can't afford here. Not even yourself."

Hinadori nodded, his throat suddenly dry as sun-baked clay. "What about you? Will I see you again?"

Something flickered in Saito's eyes... an emotion Hinadori couldn't quite pin down. Regret? Anticipation? But it vanished faster than morning dew, replaced by that same impenetrable mask.

"Sooner than you would expect." Saito said simply. Then he paused, weighing his next words like gold on a merchant's scale. "Hinadori. The path you've chosen... it'll bleed you dry. There'll be moments when you curse the day you set foot in this place, when the pain and doubt gnaw at you like hungry rats. When that happens, remember this: the Bushido Academy forges more than just warriors. It forges destiny itself."

With those cryptic words hanging in the air like storm clouds, Saito turned on his heel and strode away, leaving Hinadori alone at the foot of the imposing structure.

For a long moment, Hinadori stood frozen, the weight of his decision crashing over him like a tsunami. He thought of Noke, of the life he'd left behind. Had he made the right choice? Or had he just signed his own death warrant?

A gong sounded, its deep resonance rattling Hinadori's bones. From within the keep, a figure emerged... a severe-looking woman in robes of deepest indigo, her face etched with lines of wisdom and something harder.

"New one," she called out, her voice sharp enough to draw blood. "You there. Your first test begins now. Follow me."

Hinadori took a deep breath. Whatever lay ahead, he'd face it head-on. He'd chosen this path, and by all the gods, he'd see it through – even if it killed him.

With one last glance at the world he was leaving behind, Hinadori stepped forward into his new life at the Bushido Academy. The great doors of the keep swung shut behind him with a boom that echoed with a boom that threatened to shake the ancient gods from their celestial thrones.

As Hinadori followed the woman deeper into the keep, the air grew thick with incense and whispered secrets. They climbed endless staircases, passed through halls adorned with murals depicting epic battles and mythical beasts. Finally, they came to a stop before a set of doors so massive they made Hinadori feel like an insect.

The woman turned to him, her eyes boring into his soul. "Beyond these doors lies the Chamber. The masters await you, Hinadori of Tuchi Market. Step forward and face your destiny."

Hinadori's heart hammered against his ribs like a caged bird. This was it. The moment that would define everything. With a deep breath, he pushed open the doors and stepped into the unknown.

His eyes widened in shock as they fell upon the gathered masters.

There, seated among them in robes of authority, was Saito.

Chapter 2- The Dragon's Judgment

Hinadori's jaw dropped as his eyes locked onto the familiar figure seated at the center of the Chamber. Saito, the gruff samurai who had guided him here, now sat adorned in the ornate robes of the Grand Master. The transformation was as jarring as a slap to the face.

"Welcome, Hinadori of Tuchi Market," Saito's voice rang out, colder and more formal than Hinadori had ever heard it. "You stand before the Chamber. Speak your name and purpose."

Sooner than you'd expect? Hinadori thought, remembering what Saito had said only moments before. *Well, 'sooner' was right...*

Struggling to find his voice, Hinadori managed a shaky bow. "I... I am Hinadori, a former street rat of Tuchi Market. I seek the path of the samurai, to serve and protect."

Master Ryugen smiled with amusement as he regarded the young street rat, his demeanor surprisingly gentle compared to the other men around him.

"So, this is another young one who seeks our counsel," rumbled an elderly man next to Saito. His long white beard flowed over robes adorned with intricate dragon scales. His golden eyes sparkled with vitality as he continued, "I am Master Ryugen, though some call me the Dragon."

A muscular man with a closely-shaved head and a prominent scar on his left cheek leaned forward. "Ryugen, old friend, you're being too soft. Boy, I am Master Toramaru, and you'd do well to remember it." He flexed his fingers, reminding Saito of a tiger unsheathing its claws.

"Enough!" came a melodious voice from Saito's left. He turned to see a woman with long black hair adorned with feathers. Her ageless face bore a serene expression as she spoke. "We're here to guide, not intimidate. I am Master Tsuruko, young one."

Before Saito could respond, a deep growl emanated from the far end of the chamber.

"Test him. Now." boomed a massive man with a thick beard, his scowl visible even through the facial hair. "I am Master Kumayama, and I care little for your name, boy. Show us your worth with actions, not words."

Hinadori swallowed hard, realizing he was in the presence of the legendary masters: the Dragon, the Tiger, the Crane, and the Bear. Each introduction had given him a glimpse into their personalities, and he knew the real challenge was only beginning.

Master Ryugen leaned forward, his golden eyes seeming to pierce right through Hinadori. "Tell us, young Hinadori, what makes you think you are worthy of such an honor?"

Hinadori straightened, trying to channel the street-smart bravado that had kept him alive for so long. "I may come from nothing, Master Ryugen, but I've seen both the cruelty and kindness this world has to offer. I've survived where others have fallen. And I've learned that true strength comes not from dominating others, but from protecting those who cannot protect themselves."

Master Toramaru snorted derisively. "Pretty words. But words mean nothing here. It is action that defines a samurai."

"Master Toramaru," Hinadori said, his voice quiet but firm, "I didn't just use my words to make it past the gates. I chose to sacrifice everything I have ever known to get on this path.

"And yet," Master Tsuruko interjected, her voice soft but carrying an undercurrent of steel, "you did not come alone, did you? Tell us of your companion, the girl called Nokemono."

Hinadori hesitated, unsure of how much to reveal. He glanced at Saito, hoping for some hint of guidance, but the Grand Master's face remained impassive.

"Noke was... is... my friend," Hinadori said carefully.

Master Kumayama's eyes narrowed. ""And what of the dagger she once carried? The one Saito has returned to its rightful place?"

The question caught Hinadori off guard.

"I... I don't know much about the dagger," he admitted. "Only that it seems important to Nokemono, and that it's connected to her past somehow."

"You lie," Kumayama growled, rising to his feet. The very air seemed to vibrate with his anger. "Do not think to deceive us, boy."

Hinadori took an involuntary step back, his heart racing. "I'm not lying! I don't understand what that dagger is or why it's so important. I only know that Nokemono believes it's her destiny to wield it."

"Destiny," Master Ryugen mused, stroking his beard. "A weighty word, young Hinadori. One not to be used lightly."

Master Tsuruko tilted her head, regarding Hinadori with newfound interest. "And what of your destiny? Do you believe the winds of fate brought you here for a reason?"

Hinadori took a moment to consider his answer. "I believe... I believe that we shape our own destinies, Master Tsuruko. I chose to come here, to learn the way of the samurai. Whatever fate has in store, I intend to meet it head-on, with honor and courage."

A small smile played at the corners of Tsuruko's lips. "Well spoken."

"Bah!" Toramaru interjected. "Honor and courage are forged in battle, not flowery speeches. If the boy wants to prove himself, let him do so with steel and sweat."

"Patience, Toramaru," Ryugen cautioned. "The boy has only just arrived. There will be time enough to test his mettle."

Throughout the exchange, Saito had remained silent, observing Hinadori with an unreadable expression. Now, he leaned forward, his presence seeming to fill the entire chamber.

"You speak of honor and courage, Hinadori," Saito said, his voice carrying a new note of authority that made Hinadori's skin prickle. "But do you truly understand the weight of those words? The Bushido Academy is not the Shugendo temple. We do not coddle our students with talk of spiritual enlightenment and harmony with nature. Here, we forge warriors through fire and pain."

Hinadori swallowed hard, but met Saito's gaze. "I understand, Grand Master. I'm prepared for whatever challenges lie ahead."

A cold smile played at the corners of Saito's mouth. "Are you?" He turned to the other masters. "What say you? Shall we give this street rat a chance to prove his worth?"

Master Kumayama grunted. "I say we test him now. See if there's any steel beneath all that cunning word bending."

"And risk breaking him before he's even begun his training?" Master Tsuruko countered. "No, let him start as all students do. The Academy's trials will reveal his true nature soon enough."

Master Ryugen nodded slowly. "I agree with Tsuruko. We have much to discuss in private, fellow masters. For now, let the boy begin as others have before him."

Saito's eyes locked with Hinadori's, and for a moment, the young man thought he saw a flicker of... something. Regret? Warning? But it was gone as quickly as it appeared.

"Hinadori's past is... complicated," Saito said carefully. "As is his connection to Noke. But I believe that very complication may prove valuable in the days to come."

"Speak plainly, Saito," Toramaru demanded. "What aren't you telling us?"

A tense silence fell over the chamber. Hinadori held his breath, sensing that he was on the edge of learning something crucial about his own past.

Finally, Saito spoke.

"The threads of fate are tangled in ways we have yet to unravel. Hinadori's presence here may be more significant than any of us realize."

Hinadori's mind reeled.

What did Saito mean?

What does he know about my past that I don't myself?

Before he could voice any of these questions, Master Ryugen raised a hand, silencing the room. "Enough. We have heard what we needed to hear. Hinadori, step forward."

On shaky legs, Hinadori approached the dais. The Dragon Master's eyes seemed to bore into his very soul.

"You stand at a crossroads, young one," Ryugen said, his voice taking on an almost mystical quality. "The path you have chosen is not an easy one. It will demand everything you have and more. You will be broken down and rebuilt. Your limits will be tested, your resolve challenged. Many have tried to walk this path and failed."

Hinadori swallowed hard but met the old master's gaze steadily. "I understand, Master Ryugen."

Ryugen nodded slowly. "We shall see. For now, you are granted a place within these halls. But know this... your every action will be scrutinized. Prove yourself worthy, and you may yet become the samurai you aspire to be. Fail, and you will wish you had never left the streets of Tuchi Market."

With that ominous pronouncement, the Chamber Masters rose as one. Hinadori felt the weight of their combined gaze pressing down on him like a physical force.

"Go now," Saito commanded. "Your training begins at dawn. I suggest you use what little time you have left to prepare yourself for the trials ahead."

As Hinadori turned to leave, Saito's voice stopped him. "One last thing, Hinadori."

He looked back, finding the Grand Master's eyes fixed upon him with an intensity that made him shiver.

"Remember why you came here," Saito said, his voice resonating through the chamber with an otherworldly power that only Hinadori could hear. "The path ahead will test you in ways you cannot imagine. But never forget – you carry with you the strength of those who came before."

Hinadori's eyes widened in shock. How did Saito know about his mother? About Omo? But before he could ask, Saito had already turned away, engaged in quiet conversation with the other Chamber Masters.

Dazed, Hinadori made his way out of the Chamber hall. The morning mist had burned away, leaving the world sharp and clear. But for Hinadori, everything felt more uncertain than ever.

As he descended the stairs, his mind raced. The cryptic words of the Chamber Masters, Saito's hidden knowledge, the mysterious connection between himself and Noke – it all swirled together in a dizzying mix of confusion and anticipation.

One thing was clear... His journey at the Bushido Academy was only just beginning. And if the intensity of this first encounter with the Chamber was any indication, it would be a path fraught with danger, mystery, and the potential for greatness.

Hinadori took a deep breath, steeling himself for what was to come. Whatever lay ahead, he would face it head-on. For himself, for Noke, and for all those who believed in him – even if he didn't fully understand why.

Chapter 3 - The Dance of Steel

The first rays of dawn crept through the thin paper walls of Hinadori's *kūkan*, painting the sparse room in a pale, ghostly light. He blinked awake and sat up on the thin *tatami* mat that served as his bed.

His new living quarters were a far cry from the streets of Tuchi Market. The room was small, barely large enough for his sleeping mat and a low writing desk. A single scroll hung on the wall, bearing a calligraphy inscription that read: *"Kurushimi o tōshite tsuyosa o eru"* - Strength through suffering. Hinadori snorted. The Bushido Academy certainly seemed committed to that philosophy.

A soft scraping sound drew his attention to the door. Someone had left a tray outside. Hinadori's stomach growled as he slid the *shoji* screen aside, but his hopes for a hearty meal were quickly dashed. The tray held a small bowl of watery rice gruel, a chunk of dried fish that looked about as appetizing as shoe leather, and a cup of bitter green tea.

"Guess luxury isn't part of the samurai way," Hinadori muttered, forcing down the meager breakfast. As he choked down the last of the fish, a sharp rap on his door made him jump.

"Hinadori-san," a clipped voice called out. "Your presence is required."

He slid the door open to find a stern-faced woman in simple robes standing before him. Her graying hair was pulled back in a severe bun, and her eyes held all the warmth of a midwinter blizzard.

"I am Yuki, the *jochū* of this dormitory," she said, her tone making it clear she found the task of dealing with new recruits about as pleasant as scrubbing chamber pots. "You will address me as Yuki-san. Your first training session begins shortly with Master Swordsman Kaito. Follow me."

Without waiting for a response, Yuki turned on her heel and strode away. Hinadori scrambled to keep up, his legs still stiff from yesterday's grueling climb to the academy.

As they walked, Hinadori's mind drifted to Noke. *Where was she now? What trials was she facing at the Shugendo temple?*

Yuki's voice cut through his reverie. "Pay attention, boy. Daydreaming will get you killed here."

They had arrived at a vast courtyard, ringed by cherry trees whose delicate blossoms seemed at odds with the grim purpose of the place. Racks of wooden practice swords lined one wall, while ornate katanas and other bladed weapons hung on display, a reminder of the deadly art these students sought to master.

A group of about a dozen trainees were already gathered, their excited chatter dying down as Hinadori approached. He felt their eyes on him, sizing him up, looking for weakness.

A lean young man with perfectly coiffed hair stepped forward, his fine silk robes a stark contrast to Hinadori's simple cotton garb. "Well, well," he drawled, "if it isn't the gutter rat Saito-sama dragged in. I'm Daiki, son of the great *daimyo* Hideki. And you are...?"

Hinadori bristled at the insult but kept his voice level. "Hinadori. From Tuchi Market."

A derisive laugh rang out. "Tuchi Market? Isn't that where all the *thieves* congregate?" The speaker was a hulking mountain of a man, his arms corded with muscle and his face a mass of scar tissue. "Name's Hano. Remember it, 'cause it'll be the last thing you hear before I pound you into the dirt."

"Boys," a silky voice interjected. A graceful figure stepped forward, her movements as fluid as a stream over smooth stones. She continued, her voice carrying the quiet authority of a summer breeze, "perhaps we should welcome our new companion with honor, not hostility. I am Rin, and I believe true strength lies in both mind and body."

Daiki scowled at her. "Watch your tongue, Rin. Your family might be respected tacticians, but out here, it's strength that matters."

"Is that so?" Rin's smile never wavered. "Funny, I could have sworn it was skill and strategy that won battles, not just swinging a big stick."

Hano took a menacing step forward. "You wanna test that theory, little girl?"

Rin's eyes glinted dangerously. "Oh, I'd love to, you overgrown ox. But I prefer to save my energy for opponents who can actually think and fight at the same time. You know, a real challenge."

The tension in the air was thick enough to cut with a knife, but before things could escalate further, a commanding voice boomed across the courtyard.

"Enough!"

The students immediately fell silent, snapping to attention as a figure emerged from the shadows of the dojo. Master Swordsman Kaito was not a large man, but he carried himself with the quiet confidence of someone who knew they could end you in the blink of an eye. His weathered face was a map of old scars, and his eyes held the sharp glint of honed steel.

"If you have energy for squabbling," Kaito said, his voice as smooth and cold as ice, "then clearly I've been too soft on you. Everyone, grab a *bokken* and form up. You too, new blood."

Hinadori hurried to comply, snatching up one of the wooden practice swords. It felt awkward and heavy in his hands, nothing like the makeshift weapons he'd wielded on the streets.

"Now then," Kaito continued, pacing before the lined-up students. "Today, we drill the basics. And by basics, I mean the hundred forms of Seinaru Kaze-ryū. You will perform each form perfectly, or you will do it again. And again. And again. Until your arms fall off or you get it right. Whichever comes first."

A collective groan rose from the students, quickly silenced by Kaito's withering glare.

"Oh, I'm sorry," he said, voice dripping with sarcasm. "I thought you were here to become samurai, not whining children. Shall I fetch your wet nurses instead?"

Daiki stepped forward, bowing low. "Forgive us, Kaito-sensei. We are honored to learn from you."

Kaito's eyes narrowed. "Save your bootlicking for someone who cares, Daiki. Now, the first form. Begin!"

What followed was hours of grueling, repetitive drills.

The first form of *Seinaru Kaze-ryū-* "Embracing Wind," seemed simple enough: a smooth draw of the sword, followed by a series of fluid cuts that mimicked the flow of a gentle breeze. But as Hinadori soon discovered, simplicity did not equal ease.

His arms trembled with exertion as he attempted to maintain the precise angle of his blade. Sweat stung his eyes and trickled down his back, making his thin cotton shirt cling uncomfortably to his skin. The wooden bokken, initially just awkward, now felt like a lead weight in his blistering hands.

Nearby, Daiki moved through the *kata* with practiced ease, his movements as precise and graceful as a dancer's. "Excellent form, Daiki," Kaito nodded approvingly. "Your father's training shows."

Daiki preened at the praise, shooting a smug look in Hinadori's direction. "Thank you, Kaito-sensei. I've been practicing this form since I could walk."

"Then perhaps it's time we challenge you further," Kaito said, his voice carrying a hint of steel that made Daiki's confidence waver.

Then- "No, no, NO!" Kaito's voice cracked like a whip.

The master swordsman seemed to materialize beside Hinadori, his own practice sword a blur as it rapped sharply against Hinadori's wrists, forcing his stance wider. "Your feet are all wrong. Wider stance, deeper bend in the knees. You're not lounging in a tea house, boy!"

Hinadori bit back a yelp of pain, quickly adjusting his posture. But no sooner had he done so than Kaito was behind him, delivering a stinging blow to his lower back.

"Straighten that spine! You look like a hunchbacked beggar, not a samurai!"

As Hinadori struggled to maintain his form, he caught sight of Rin out of the corner of his eye. Unlike Daiki's showy precision or Hano's brute force approach, Rin moved with a calculated efficiency. Each motion was crisp and purposeful, wasting no energy.

Kaito observed her for a moment before offering a curt nod. *"Bōgen,"* he said simply, the admiration behind the word hanging in the air. "The rest of you would do well to observe her efficiency."

Daiki's face darkened at this, his next few swings becoming overly aggressive as he tried to recapture Kaito's attention.

On Hinadori's left, Hano grunted with exertion, his massive frame struggling to achieve the fluidity the *kata* demanded. His movements were powerful but clumsy, like a bear trying to perform a butterfly's dance.

"Hano!" Kaito barked. "This isn't a contest to see who can chop the most wood! Finesse, boy, finesse!"

Hano's face reddened with a mix of embarrassment and anger. "Yes, Kaito-sensei," he growled through gritted teeth.

Every time Hinadori thought he'd grasped the form, Kaito found another flaw to correct. A misaligned elbow here, an improperly angled wrist there. Each mistake was met with a sharp word and an even sharper strike from Kaito's bokken.

"Pathetic, street rat," Kaito growled after correcting Hinadori's stance for the dozenth time. "My grandmother could perform this *kata* better, and she's been dead for thirty years."

Snickers rose from the other students, particularly Daiki and his cronies. Hinadori gritted his teeth, forcing himself to focus on the movements rather than the jeers. He could feel their eyes on him, hungry for any sign of weakness.

As the sun climbed higher in the sky, Hinadori's arms felt like lead weights. His palms were raw and blistered from gripping the bokken, every movement sending fresh jolts of pain through his hands. Yet still, Kaito drove them on, relentless in his pursuit of perfection.

"Again!" he barked. "And this time, try not to embarrass yourselves and dishonor your ancestors."

Hinadori's mind drifted as his body moved through the now-familiar motions. He thought of Noke, of the Wind of Death, of the cryptic words the Chamber had spoken. There was so much he didn't understand, so many secrets swirling around him.

Another sharp crack across his shoulders snapped him back to reality.

"Wake up, boy!" Kaito snarled. "Your mind wanders, and in battle, that means death. Do you want to die, Hinadori?"

Hinadori straightened, meeting Kaito's fierce gaze. "No, sensei."

"Then prove it. Show me you have what it takes to be here, or go back to the gutters where you belong."

Something inside Hinadori withered at those words.

He might not have the noble upbringing of Daiki or the tactical genius of Rin, but he had survived things these pampered students couldn't imagine. He'd clawed his way out of poverty and desperation to stand here. He wouldn't let anyone, not Kaito, not his rivals, not even his own doubts, drag him back down.

With renewed determination, Hinadori threw himself into the drills. He shut out everything else... the pain, the exhaustion, the mocking laughter of his peers. There was only the sword, the movement, the flow of energy from his core to the tip of the blade.

His movements were far from perfect, but there was a raw intensity to them now, a stubborn refusal to yield. Where before he had been stiff and hesitant, now there was a fluid grace born of desperation and sheer willpower. The *bokken* became an extension of his arm, cutting through the air with a soft whisper that spoke of growing confidence.

As the grueling session finally came to an end, Hinadori caught a fleeting look of... something in Kaito's eyes.

Not approval, exactly, but perhaps a grudging acknowledgment.

"Dismissed," Kaito barked. "Rest up. Tomorrow, we see if any of you can actually use those toothpicks in a real fight."

As the students filed out, Hinadori was shoved to the side. Turning, he saw Daiki moving past him, barely looking in Hinadori's direction.

"Don't get too comfortable," Daiki hissed. "Your kind doesn't last long here. Soon enough, you'll be back in the gutter where you belong."

Rin and Hano laughed as they followed Daiki out of sight.

Hinadori blinked.

Exhausted and sore, he lingered for a moment.

He stared at the ornate katanas on display, their polished blades catching the late afternoon sun.

One day, he vowed silently, he would prove himself worthy of wielding such a weapon.

One day, he would show them all what a "street rat" could do.

With that thought burning in his mind, Hinadori trudged back to his *kūkan*, his body aching but his spirit unbroken.

The real test, he knew, was only just beginning.

Chapter 4- Stringing Fate

D awn broke over the Bushido Academy again, painting the sky in hues of pink and gold.

Hinadori's body ached from yesterday's grueling sword training as he made his way to the archery range, a sprawling field dotted with straw targets at varying distances. A light mist clung to the ground, giving the scene an almost ethereal quality.

As the students gathered, a figure emerged from the early morning haze. Archery Instructor Yumi moved with a grace that seemed almost supernatural, her long black hair adorned with a single white crane feather. Her eyes, sharp as an eagle's, surveyed the assembled trainees.

"Welcome," Yumi said, her voice calm yet carrying an undercurrent of steel. "Today, you will learn the art of *kyūdō*. The way of the bow is not merely about hitting a target. It is about harmonizing your body, mind, and spirit."

She demonstrated the proper stance, her movements fluid and precise. "Observe. The draw is not just in your arms, but in your entire being. You must become one with the bow, with the arrow, with the very air around you."

As Yumi distributed the *yumi-* bows and *ya-* arrows, Hinadori couldn't help but notice how different they felt from the crude weapons he'd cobbled together on the streets. These were works of art, each bow a masterpiece of laminated bamboo and wood.

Daiki stepped up first, a confident smirk playing on his lips. He rolled his shoulders, making a show of loosening up as he approached the firing line. His silk robes rustled softly as he moved, a reminder of his noble status even here on the practice field.

"Watch and learn," he murmured to the others, loud enough for Hinadori to hear. "This is how a true samurai handles a bow."

Daiki's posture was textbook perfect as he knocked the arrow. His back straight, shoulders aligned, he drew the string back with practiced ease. His face was a mask of concentration, eyes narrowed as he sighted down the arrow shaft.

For a moment, he held the pose, a living statue of archery form. Then, with a soft exhalation, he released. The arrow flew true, cutting through the morning air with a soft whistle.

It struck the target, and Daiki's smirk widened into a full grin. But as the other trainees craned their necks to see, that grin faltered.

The arrow had indeed hit the target... but only on the outer ring, far from the bullseye Daiki had clearly been aiming for.

"Not bad, Daiki," Yumi said, her tone neutral. "But you are too rigid. The bow is not an enemy to be conquered, but a partner in the dance."

Daiki's face flushed red, a mix of embarrassment and anger. "But Yumi-sensei," he protested, "my form was perfect. Just as my father taught me."

Yumi's gaze sharpened. "Perfect form without spirit is like a beautiful sword without an edge. Useless in battle." She stepped closer, adjusting Daiki's stance with firm but gentle hands. "You must learn to bend like the bamboo, Daiki. Strong, yet flexible. Your noble upbringing has made you stiff. You must unlearn this if you wish to truly master the bow."

Daiki's jaw clenched, his eyes flashing with humiliation as snickers rose from the other trainees. He bowed stiffly to Yumi, but as he stepped back into line, Hinadori caught the look of pure venom Daiki shot his way. It was clear the young noble was not used to being anything less than the best, and he'd remember this slight for a long time to come.

Hano went next, his massive frame dwarfing the elegant bow. He drew with too much force, the bow creaking ominously. His arrow sailed far over the target, disappearing into the misty field beyond.

"Power without control is worse than useless, Hano," Yumi admonished. "You must learn finesse."

Rin's attempt was more successful. Her arrow struck just left of center, a respectable showing for a first attempt. Yumi nodded approvingly but offered no verbal praise.

Finally, it was Hinadori's turn. He stepped up to the line, acutely aware of the eyes boring into his back. The bow felt awkward in his hands, nothing like the wooden swords from yesterday. He took a deep breath, trying to recall Yumi's instructions.

To his surprise, as he knocked the arrow and drew back, something clicked.

The stance felt... right. Natural, even. He focused on the target, letting the world fall away until there was nothing but him, the bow, and the distant circle of straw.

The arrow flew, cutting through the morning mist with a soft whisper. It struck dead center with a satisfying *thunk*.

A hush fell over the training ground.

Hinadori blinked, hardly believing what he'd just done.

Yumi's eyebrows rose slightly, the most expression anyone had seen on her face all morning.

"Well," she said, a hint of surprise in her voice, "it seems our new recruit has a natural affinity for the bow. Well done, Hinadori."

Shocked and envious murmurs rippled through the other trainees. Daiki's face darkened with barely concealed rage, while Hano cracked his knuckles menacingly. Only Rin seemed more intrigued than angry, studying Hinadori with newfound interest.

The rest of the morning passed in a blur of instruction and practice. By the time Yumi called for a break, Hinadori's fingers were raw and his shoulders ached, but a small spark of pride had kindled in his chest.

As the trainees made their way to a nearby pavilion for lunch, Hinadori found himself alone, the others giving him a wide berth. He sat cross-legged on the worn wooden floor, unwrapping the skimpy meal provided... a small ball of cold rice, a strip of dried seaweed, and a few pickled vegetables.

"Bet the street rat's used to scrape like this," Daiki's voice carried across the pavilion, loud enough to ensure Hinadori would hear. "Probably thinks he's dining like an emperor."

Hano's deep chuckle followed. "Maybe that's his secret. Can't shoot straight if you're weighed down by real food."

"Or maybe," Rin's cool voice cut in, "he's just better than you. Imagine that."

Hinadori kept his head down, focusing on his food and trying to ignore the barbed words. He'd endured worse on the streets of Tuchi Market. Still, the isolation stung more than he cared to admit.

After the all-too-brief respite, training resumed. The afternoon sun beat down mercilessly as the trainees continued to hone their skills. Hinadori's initial success proved to be no fluke. While not every shot was perfect, his arrows consistently found their mark more often than not.

As the day wore on, even Yumi's stoic demeanor began to show cracks of approval.

"Your form is improving, Hinadori," she noted after a particularly impressive series of shots. "You have a gift. Now we must work to refine it."

Finally, as the sun dipped low on the horizon, Yumi called an end to the session.

"You've all made progress today," she said, her gaze sweeping over the exhausted trainees. "But there is still much to learn. Hinadori."

He looked up, startled at being singled out.

"Your performance today was... unexpected," Yumi continued. "You have a rare talent. Nurture it well. It may serve you better than you know in the days to come."

With that cryptic remark, she turned and glided away, leaving Hinadori to ponder her words.

As the trainees began to disperse, the whispers started.

"Teacher's pet," someone hissed.

"Beginner's luck," another voice growled.

"Won't last," a third chimed in.

Hinadori squared his shoulders, ignoring the jealous mutters. For the first time since arriving at the Academy, he felt a glimmer of hope. He may not have Daiki's noble upbringing or Hano's brute strength, but he had found something he was truly good at.

As he made his way back to his kūkan, bow in hand, Hinadori allowed himself a small smile. The path ahead was still long and fraught with challenges, but now he knew he had it in him to face them.

One arrow at a time, he would prove himself worthy of standing among the samurai.

Chapter 5- Fists of Fury, Heart of Fire

The gong's resonant boom shattered Hinadori's fitful sleep, its echo seeming to reverberate through his very bones.

For a disorienting moment, he was back in Tuchi Market, diving for cover at the sound of the city watch's alarm. But reality crashed back as his eyes focused on the austere walls of his kūkan.

A voice drifted through the thin walls, carried on the pre-dawn air. It was Yuki, the *jochū*, her tone clipped and impatient as always.

"Up, all of you! The sun does not wait, nor shall your training!"

Hinadori winced as he pushed himself upright, his body a symphony of aches. His fingers ghosted over his palms, feeling the tender blisters from yesterday's archery practice, the first signs of calluses beginning to form beneath. A fleeting smile crossed his face at the memory of his unexpected success, but it quickly faded. One small victory didn't change the fact that he was still an outsider here, tolerated at best, despised at worst.

As he stumbled to his feet, a slip of paper caught his eye. It had been slid under his door sometime in the night. Curious, Hinadori unfolded it, his breath catching as he read the message scrawled in hasty charcoal:

"Watch your back, street rat. Your beginner's luck won't save you today."

The words were unsigned, but Hinadori could practically hear Daiki's sneering voice in every stroke. He crumpled the note, a mix of anger and determination hardening in his gut. If they thought to intimidate him, they'd soon learn how little effect such threats had on someone who'd grown up dodging knives in dark alleys.

Yuki's sharp rap on his door interrupted his thoughts. "Hinadori! Hand-to-hand combat training. Now."

He slid the door open, meeting Yuki's icy stare with a calm he didn't entirely feel. "Lead the way, Yuki-san."

As they walked, Hinadori noticed something different in the air.

A tension, an anticipation that seemed to charge the very atmosphere of the Academy. Other trainees hurried past, their faces a mix of excitement and apprehension. Whispered conversations died as he approached, replaced by pointed looks and poorly concealed smirks.

"Yuki-san," Hinadori ventured, curiosity overcoming his usual reticence, "what's going on? Everyone seems... on edge."

Yuki's pace didn't slow and she did not address his question.

Rather, she explained, "Today you meet Akio-sensei. The hand-to-hand combat specialist." She paused, then added, "Some say he's the most dangerous man in the Academy. Even the other masters tread carefully around him."

Hinadori's stomach tightened. "More dangerous than Kaito-sensei?"

A humorless chuckle escaped Yuki's lips. "Kaito can kill you with a sword. Akio? He can kill you with his bare hands. And some whisper... he enjoys it a little too much."

With those ominous words hanging in the air, they arrived at a large, open-air dojo nestled between two imposing stone buildings. The floor was covered in tightly woven tatami mats, their fresh scent mingling with the morning air. Wooden dummy posts lined one wall, their surfaces scarred and splintered from countless blows.

As Hinadori entered, the other trainees instantly shifted away, leaving a conspicuous empty space around him. Daiki and his cronies huddled together, shooting venomous glares his way. Even Rin, who had shown a hint of approval yesterday, kept her distance. The message was clear: Hinadori's unexpected success with the bow had only served to isolate him further.

A hush fell over the dojo, the tension ratcheting up to an almost unbearable level. Then, without warning, a figure burst through the doors, moving so fast it seemed to materialize out of thin air in the center of the room.

Hand-to-Hand Combat Specialist Akio stood before them, his presence filling the space like a storm cloud about to break. He was shorter than Hinadori had expected, but built like a coiled spring, every inch of him radiating lethal potential. Scars criss crossed his bare arms and face, telling tales of countless battles survived.

Akio's eyes, sharp as a hawk's, swept over the assembled students. When they landed on Hinadori, a small, predatory smile curved his lips. He cocked his head, studying Hinadori with unnerving intensity. Then, he whispered so quietly that only Hinadori could hear, "Let's see if you're as quick with your fists as you are with a bow, shall we?"

Hinadori swallowed hard before Akio straightened and addressed the rest of the trainees.

"Listen up," Akio's voice boomed, filling the space. "I'm not here to coddle you or hold your hands. By the time I'm done with you, your bodies will be weapons deadlier than any sword."

He launched into a demonstration, his movements a blur of controlled violence. "Today, we focus on three basic moves: the hammer fist, the palm heel strike, and the elbow smash. Watch closely. I won't repeat myself."

Akio's voice cut through the tension like a blade. "Pay attention, weaklings. I'll demonstrate each technique once. Miss it, and you'll learn through pain instead."

He moved to the center of the dojo, his stance low and predatory. "First, the hammer fist. Simple, brutal, effective."

Akio's fist blurred through the air, stopping a hair's breadth from a wooden dummy's head. The impact would have been devastating had he followed through.

"Pair up and practice. Now!"

The students scrambled to find partners. Hinadori found himself face-to-face with Daiki, the noble's lips curled in a sneer.

"Try not to embarrass yourself, street rat," Daiki hissed as they got into their fighting stances.

Hinadori's first attempts at the hammer fist were clumsy, his strikes lacking power. Daiki, on the other hand, executed the move with practiced ease.

"Pathetic," Daiki taunted after easily deflecting another of Hinadori's strikes. "Did you learn to fight from a drunken geisha?"

Gritting his teeth, Hinadori redoubled his efforts, but Daiki's superior training was evident.

Akio's voice boomed again. "Enough! Next technique: palm heel strike. Watch closely."

This time, Akio demonstrated a vicious upward strike that could shatter a nose or crush a windpipe. As the students paired off again, Hinadori found himself facing Rin.

Her eyes were lifeless as she sized him up, like a cobra ready to strike. "Don't think your archery skills mean anything here, Hinadori. This is where real warriors prove themselves."

They began practicing the palm heel strike. Rin's movements were precise and calculated, each strike stopping just short of actual contact. Hinadori, still struggling with the technique, accidentally connected one of his strikes, causing Rin to stumble back.

"Watch it, you clumsy oaf!" she spat, her earlier neutrality evaporating. "Can't you control your own body?"

"I'm sorry, I didn't mean to—" Hinadori began, but Rin cut him off with a lightning-fast palm strike that grazed his chin, leaving it stinging.

"Oops," she said, her voice dripping with false innocence. "Guess I can't control my body either."

Before Hinadori could respond, Akio called for attention once more. "Last basic technique: the elbow smash. Devastating in close quarters."

He demonstrated, his elbow cutting through the air with frightening speed and precision. As the students moved to practice, Hinadori found himself paired with Hano, the hulking trainee's eyes glinting with malice.

"Been looking forward to this, runt," Hano growled, cracking his knuckles menacingly.

They began drilling the elbow smash, and Hinadori immediately felt the difference. Where Daiki and Rin had at least maintained the pretense of practice, Hano seemed intent on doing real damage. His "practice" strikes came dangerously close to full force, each one feeling like it might shatter Hinadori's bones.

Hano's massive fist connected with Hinadori's solar plexus with such force that Hinadori felt his heart skip a beat, a brush with what seemed like death itself.

Gritting his teeth, Hinadori launched himself at Hano, landing a flurry of strikes that the larger trainee barely seemed to notice. Hano's laughter boomed through the dojo, making Hinadori feel small and insignificant.

"Is that all you've got, street rat?" Hano taunted, easily deflecting another of Hinadori's attacks. "Come on, fight back! Or are you only tough when you've got a bow in your hands?"

Hinadori tried to give as good as he got, but Hano's size and strength advantage was overwhelming. By the time Akio called for them to stop, Hinadori was covered in sweat and bruises, his breath coming in ragged gasps.

As he struggled to catch his breath, Hinadori couldn't help but notice the satisfied smirks on his fellow trainees' faces. It was clear that in this arena, at least, they felt they had put the upstart street rat back in his place.

Little did they know, their actions were only stoking the fire of Hinadori's determination. He may have been outmatched today, but he silently vowed to master these techniques, no matter the cost. The day would come when he'd wipe those smug looks off their faces, one way or another.

Just as the grueling session seemed to be winding down, Akio's voice cut through the air like a whip crack. "Daiki! Front and center."

The noble's son swaggered forward, a cocky grin plastered on his face. "Ready to learn from the master, sensei?"

Akio's eyes narrowed. "Attack me. Don't hold back."

What followed was a blur of motion. Daiki launched a flurry of strikes, each more vicious than the last. It was clear he wasn't just sparring – he was trying to hurt Akio, to prove his superiority.

For a moment, it seemed Akio was on the defensive. Then, faster than Hinadori's eyes could follow, the master struck. There was no wasted motion, no flashy technique. Just three precise strikes, and Daiki crumpled to the floor, gasping for air.

Akio turned to address the stunned class, his voice low and deadly serious. "What you just witnessed is a technique not to be used lightly. In fact, outside of mortal combat, it is forbidden."

The air seemed to thicken with tension as Akio demonstrated a lightning-fast series of strikes targeting specific points on the body.

"This," he growled, "is the *Koroshi no Ichigeki*- Killing Blow. It disrupts the body's vital energy flows, capable of downing even the strongest opponent. But make no mistake... used improperly, it can cripple or kill."

Hinadori watched, transfixed, as Akio's hands danced through the air, miming the deadly technique. Something about the move resonated deep within him, as if awakening a dormant instinct.

"I will say it again. Engrain this into your mind: this technique is forbidden for a reason." Akio's eyes bored into each student in turn, lingering a moment longer on Hinadori, "I show it to you not to use, but to defend against. Understood?"

A chorus of "*Hai*, sensei!" echoed through the dojo.

...

The moon hung low in the sky, casting long shadows across the Academy grounds. Hinadori's feet carried him aimlessly, his mind a whirlwind of doubts and determination. He found himself at the edge of a small koi pond, its waters dark and still in the night.

After training had ended for the day, the trainees gathered for another space meal, the bland food barely enough to satisfy their hunger. The air was filled with laughter as the others chatted and shared stories, but Hinadori felt an overwhelming sense of isolation. While his peers exchanged jokes and boisterous banter, he quietly slipped away, feeling unwelcome among them.

Sitting alone in his quarters, he tried to shake off the discomfort, but restlessness gnawed at him. He could not bear to remain still any longer, so he decided to take a walk.

Now, Hinadori stared at his reflection, barely recognizing the face that looked back at him. How far he'd come from the streets of Tuchi Market.

And yet, how far he still had to go.

Then, a sharp pain suddenly blossomed at the back of his head.

Hinadori whirled around, his hand instinctively reaching for the spot where something had struck him. A small pebble clattered to the ground at his feet.

"Well, well," a familiar voice drawled from the shadows. "If it isn't the Academy's pet street rat."

Daiki emerged from behind a nearby cherry tree, his usually immaculate appearance slightly disheveled. His eyes glinted with malice in the moonlight.

"Daiki," Hinadori acknowledged, keeping his voice level. "Isn't it past your bedtime?"

Daiki's face twisted into a sneer. "You dare speak to me like that? You, who don't even deserve to breathe the same air as the rest of us?"

Hinadori felt his temper flare but fought to keep it in check. "We're all students here, Daiki. The Academy chose me, same as you."

"Chose you?" Daiki spat. "They let you in out of pity, nothing more. You're a stain on this institution's honor."

"And you think your noble blood makes you worthy?" Hinadori shot back, his patience wearing thin. "I've earned my place here through grit and determination. What have you done besides ride your family's coattails?"

Daiki's face flushed with rage. He closed the distance between them in two quick strides, grabbing Hinadori by the front of his shirt. "I ought to beat that insolence out of you right here and now."

Hinadori's mind raced. He was exhausted from the day's training, and Daiki's superior physical conditioning gave him a clear advantage.

But maybe...

"Go ahead," Hinadori said, forcing a smirk. "Show everyone how the great Daiki fights. Attacking someone in the dead of night, with no witnesses. Real honorable."

Daiki's grip tightened, but Hinadori saw a flicker of uncertainty in his eyes.

"Or," Hinadori continued, "if you're so sure of your superiority, why not prove it during sparring? In front of everyone. Unless... you're afraid?"

"Afraid?" Daiki snarled. "Of you?"

"Then what's stopping you?" Hinadori pressed. "Beat me in front of our peers, our sensei. Prove once and for all that you're better than the street rat. Unless you're a coward who only picks fights in the dark."

For a long moment, Daiki said nothing. His fingers slowly uncurled from Hinadori's shirt.

"Tomorrow," Daiki said, his voice low and dangerous. "During hand-to-hand training. I'll show everyone exactly where you belong."

With that, he turned and stalked away, leaving Hinadori alone by the koi pond once more.

Hinadori let out a shaky breath, adrenaline still coursing through his veins. He'd bought himself some time, but tomorrow's reckoning loomed large. As he made his way back to his quarters, one thought echoed in his mind...

What had he just gotten himself into?

Chapter 6- The Reckoning

*D*ONG! DUM! DONG!

The gong's resonant boom barely registered in Hinadori's consciousness. He had been awake for hours, sleep eluding him as his mind raced with thoughts of the impending confrontation with Daiki.

As he made his way to the training grounds, every shadow seemed to loom larger, every sound amplified by his frayed nerves. The usual chatter of his fellow trainees felt distant, muffled, as if he were underwater.

The morning's sword training with Kaito-sensei passed in a blur. Hinadori's usually improving form suffered, his strikes lacking their newfound precision.

"Focus, boy!" Kaito barked, rapping Hinadori's knuckles with the flat of his practice blade. "Your mind wanders, and in battle, that means death."

Hinadori nodded, forcing himself to concentrate. But even as he corrected his stance, his thoughts drifted to the hand-to-hand combat training that loomed on the horizon.

Archery practice with Yumi-sensei fared no better. His arrows, which had flown true just days before, now scattered wide of their marks.

Yumi's sharp eyes missed nothing. "Your spirit is troubled, Hinadori," she observed, her voice low enough that only he could hear. "Remember, the bow is an extension of yourself. If your mind is chaotic, so too will be your shots."

Hinadori took a deep breath, trying to center himself. He nocked another arrow, drew back, and released. This time, it struck closer to the target's center, but still far from his usual accuracy.

As the sun climbed higher in the sky, Hinadori's anxiety grew. He had managed to delay his confrontation with Daiki, but at what cost? He had only postponed the inevitable, and now he would face Daiki's wrath in front of their peers and instructors.

During the brief lunch break, Hinadori found himself unable to eat. He sat alone, picking at his meager rations, his mind racing through potential scenarios.

Could he fake an injury?

No, that would only delay things further and mark him as a coward.

Could he appeal to Akio-sensei for protection?

The very thought made him wince. Akio would sooner throw him to the wolves than intervene in a student dispute.

As the trainees began to gather for the afternoon's hand-to-hand combat session, Hinadori felt a presence at his side. He turned to find Rin studying him with those sharp, calculating eyes.

"You look like you're marching to your execution," she observed dryly.

Hinadori managed a weak smile. "That obvious, huh?"

Rin's gaze flickered to where Daiki stood with his cronies, all of them shooting venomous glares in Hinadori's direction. "Word travels fast here," she said. "I heard about your little midnight encounter."

Hinadori's heart sank. "Great. So everyone knows."

"Not everyone," Rin shrugged. "But enough. Daiki's been bragging all morning about how he's going to put you in your place."

"Any advice?" Hinadori asked, desperation creeping into his voice.

Rin was silent for a moment, her expression unreadable. Finally, she spoke. "Daiki's strong, and he's had years of training. But he's arrogant. He telegraphs his moves. Watch his shoulders.... they tense before he strikes."

Before Hinadori could respond, Akio's commanding voice cut through the air. "Today, we learn the Kaze no Tsume - Wind Claw technique. Watch closely."

Hinadori watched as Akio's hands blurred through the air, his fingers curled into claw-like shapes. The movement was fluid yet deadly, designed to target an opponent's vital points with devastating precision.

As Akio demonstrated, Hinadori felt Daiki's eyes boring into him from across the training ground. The noble's son's gaze held a promise of pain to come.

"Pair up and practice," Akio barked. "I want to see perfect form, or you'll all be doing push-ups until your arms fall off."

Before Hinadori could even think about finding a partner, Daiki was there, a predatory grin on his face. "Ready for our rematch, street rat?"

Hinadori's mouth went dry.

This was the moment he'd been dreading all day.

He knew he had no choice... backing down now would mark him as a coward in front of everyone.

"Anytime you are, Daiki," Hinadori managed, his voice steadier than he felt.

Daiki's grin widened. "Actually," he said, loud enough for the entire class to hear, "why don't we make this interesting? A real match, right here, right now. Unless you're too scared?"

The other students began to gather around, sensing the tension in the air. Hinadori could feel their eyes on him, waiting to see how he'd respond.

Taking a deep breath, Hinadori nodded. "You're on."

Akio's eyes narrowed as he observed the exchange. "Very well," he said after a moment. "If you two want to test your skills, so be it. But remember... This is training, not a blood feud. First to yield or become incapacitated loses."

Hinadori and Daiki squared off in the center of a hastily formed ring of students. Daiki cracked his knuckles, still grinning. "Last chance to back out, gutter trash."

In response, Hinadori settled into his fighting stance. His heart was pounding, but he forced himself to focus, remembering Rin's advice about watching Daiki's tells.

"Begin!" Akio's voice cracked like a whip.

Daiki wasted no time, charging forward with a flurry of strikes. Hinadori backpedaled, desperately blocking and dodging. A glancing blow caught his shoulder, sending a jolt of pain down his arm.

"Come on, fight back!" Daiki taunted, pressing his advantage. His fists whistled through the air, barely missing Hinadori's face. "Or is running away all you're good at? I guess that's what street rats do best!"

Hinadori's breath came in ragged gasps as he dodged another blow. Rin's words echoed in his mind... *Watch his shoulders... they tense before he strikes.*

He forced himself to focus, to look past the flurry of punches.

There!

Daiki's right shoulder tightened, a split second before he threw a haymaker. Hinadori ducked under the swing, feeling the wind of its passage ruffle his hair.

"Not bad, gutter trash," Daiki sneered, momentarily thrown off balance. "But dodging won't win you this fight!"

Gritting his teeth, Hinadori saw an opening and struck. His fist connected solidly with Daiki's ribs, eliciting a grunt of pain from the noble's son.

"Lucky shot," Daiki growled, his eyes narrowing. "Let's see you do that again!"

The fight continued, a brutal dance of strikes and counters. Hinadori managed to anticipate a few more of Daiki's attacks thanks to Rin's advice, but it wasn't enough. For every blow he dodged, two more seemed to slip through his guard.

"Is this the best you can do?" Daiki taunted, landing a stinging jab to Hinadori's cheek. "I've had more challenging fights with my little sister!"

Hinadori's vision blurred from the impact, but he forced himself to stay focused. He lashed out with a kick, catching Daiki in the stomach. The noble's son stumbled back a step, surprise flashing across his face before being replaced by rage.

"You'll pay for that, street rat," Daiki snarled.

As the match wore on, Hinadori felt himself tiring. His reactions were slowing, his blocks becoming sloppier. Daiki, sensing weakness, pressed harder.

"Getting tired, Hinadori?" Daiki's voice dripped with mock concern. "Don't worry, I'll put you out of your misery soon enough!"

Suddenly, Daiki's leg snaked out, hooking behind Hinadori's ankle. It was a dirty move, not part of any technique they'd been taught. Hinadori's eyes widened in shock as he felt himself losing balance.

"Wha-" was all he managed before he went down hard, the impact driving the air from his lungs.

Before he could recover, Daiki was on him, raining down blows. Hinadori curled up, trying to protect himself, but Daiki's fists seemed to find every unguarded spot.

"This is where you belong," Daiki growled between punches. "In the dirt, under my feet!"

Hinadori tried to block, to counter, but Daiki's assault was relentless. Each impact sent fresh waves of pain through his battered body.

Through swollen eyes, Hinadori caught glimpses of the crowd around them. Some were cheering Daiki on, while others watched in silent shock. He thought he saw Rin, her face a mask of concern, but then another blow snapped his head to the side.

"Had enough yet?" Daiki sneered, pausing his attack for a moment. "Just yield, and I might let you crawl away with some dignity."

Hinadori tasted blood in his mouth. Every inch of him screamed in pain. But deep inside, a spark of defiance still burned. He wouldn't give Daiki the satisfaction of breaking him.

"Is... is that all you've got?" Hinadori managed to gasp out, forcing a bloodied smile. "Even the *girl* in the class hits harder than you!"

Daiki's face contorted with fury. "You asked for it, gutter trash. I'm going to make you regret ever setting foot in this academy!"

As Daiki wound up for another devastating blow, something in Hinadori snapped. A lifetime of being looked down on, of fighting just to survive - it all came boiling to the surface in a wave of white-hot rage.

Without conscious thought, Hinadori's body moved. His hands formed the claw shape of the Kaze no Tsume, but there was something else there too... a half-remembered movement from Akio's forbidden technique demonstration.

Hinadori struck upwards with all his might, his fingers aimed at Daiki's vital points. There was a sickening impact, and Daiki's eyes went wide with shock and pain.

But something was wrong.

As Daiki stumbled backward, Hinadori felt a searing agony shoot up his arm.

It was as if he'd punched a wall of fire.

Both boys collapsed to the ground, Daiki clutching his chest and gasping for air, Hinadori cradling his mangled hand.

The training ground erupted into chaos. Students were shouting, some rushing to Daiki's side, others backing away in horror. Akio's voice boomed over the din, calling for the medical team.

As darkness began to creep in at the edges of Hinadori's vision, he caught snippets of frantic conversation.

"... punctured lung..."

"... ki pathways disrupted..."

"... might lose the hand..."

"... don't know if either will survive..."

The last thing Hinadori saw before unconsciousness claimed him was Akio's face, the master's expression a mix of anger and something that looked almost like fear.

Then, mercifully, everything went black.

Chapter 7- Breaking Hinadori

Hinadori struggled to sit up, wincing as pain lanced through his ribs. A spasm of pain shot through his body as the events of the day before came back to him.

This was his consequence for...

For what?

The memories were hazy, clouded by exhaustion and the lingering tendrils of his dream. He remembered a fight, a moment of blind rage that had overtaken him.

And then... nothing.

How had he ended up here?

More importantly, how was he going to prove himself worthy of the path he'd chosen?

With a groan, Hinadori forced himself to his feet. His legs trembled, threatening to give out beneath him. But he gritted his teeth and remained standing.

Suddenly, flashes of memory assaulted him... the feeling of his hand connecting with Daiki's chest, the sickening crunch, the white-hot agony that followed. The forbidden technique. Hinadori's stomach churned as the full weight of what he'd done crashed over him.

A harsh cough wracked his body, reminding him of his other injuries. As he steadied himself against the wall, his eyes fell upon a bowl of water on a nearby table. Its intended use was to cool his sore hands, but today he was surprised to see a reflection in the ripples.

. The face that stared back at him was barely recognizable... swollen, bruised, with a nasty gash across his left cheek that was still healing.

"What have I done?" he whispered to his distorted reflection in the bowl of water he could barely lift with his trembling hands.

As if in answer, the sound of heavy footsteps echoed from the hallway outside. Hinadori tensed, recognizing the purposeful stride of Master Toramaru. He nearly lost his grip on the bowl but managed to set it down just in time. At that exact moment, the door slid open with a sharp crack, revealing the imposing figure of the combat instructor.

Master Toramaru's face was a mask of controlled fury as he regarded Hinadori. "So, the disgrace awakens," he growled.

Hinadori opened his mouth to speak, but Toramaru cut him off with a sharp gesture.

"Save your excuses, boy. Your actions have brought shame not only upon yourself but upon this entire academy. You used a forbidden technique, one you shouldn't even know, and nearly killed a fellow student. And for what? Your pride?"

Each word hit Hinadori like a physical blow. He wanted to defend himself, to explain the provocation, the desperation he'd felt. But he knew it would fall on deaf ears.

"Master Toramaru, I-"

"Silence!" Toramaru's voice cracked like a whip. "You will speak only when spoken to. From this moment forward, you are cut off from the other students. Your training will be under my direct supervision, and it will make everything you've experienced so far seem like a pleasant dream."

Hinadori's heart sank.

Isolation.

Intensified training.

It was a punishment designed to break him.

"But Master," he ventured, "how am I supposed to learn and grow if I'm cut off from my peers?"

Toramaru's eyes narrowed dangerously. "Learn? Grow? You think you deserve such privileges after what you've done? No, Hinadori. You will learn through pain. You will grow through solitude. And perhaps, if you survive, you will emerge as something worthy of the title 'samurai.'"

With that, Toramaru turned to leave. At the doorway, he paused, looking back over his shoulder. "Your new regimen begins at dawn. I suggest you use what little time you have left to reflect on the consequences of your actions."

The door slid shut with finality, leaving Hinadori alone once more. He slumped against the wall, his mind reeling. The dream of Noke, the memory of his past life, seemed impossibly distant now. All that stretched before him was a long, dark road of suffering and solitude.

But as he looked at his bandaged hand, a spark of determination kindled in his chest. He had survived the streets of Tuchi Market. He had endured loss and hardship. He would survive this too.

Hinadori pushed himself off the wall, ignoring the protests of his battered body. He began to stretch, to prepare himself as best he could for the trials to come. Whatever Master Toramaru had in store for him, he would face it head-on.

The true test, he realized, was only just beginning.

...

A Few Hours Later

...

The sharp crack of a bamboo staff striking the floor echoed through the room, snapping Hinadori awake before the light of day touched the sky.

His eyes, heavy with exhaustion, struggled to focus on the bare walls of his isolation chamber. Every muscle in his body screamed in protest as he forced himself to sit up, the memories of yesterday's grueling training session still fresh in his mind.

"Up, boy!" Master Toramaru's voice boomed from beyond the door. "Your training begins now!"

Hinadori stumbled to his feet, his legs trembling beneath him. He had barely managed two hours of sleep, his dreams haunted by the faces of his fellow trainees... faces he hadn't seen in weeks. As he reached for his training gi, his stomach growled loudly, a painful reminder of the meager scraps that now constituted his daily meals.

Outside, the air was bitter cold, the kind that gnawed at the skin and settled deep in the bones. A thick, clinging mist hovered just above the ground, obscuring the earth beneath Hinadori's feet and making every breath feel heavier. The early morning light barely pierced the haze, and the academy grounds were silent, save for the occasional whisper of wind through the trees.

Toramaru stood at the edge of the yard, his figure like a stone statue in the gloom. His face, as always, was unreadable—a mask of hardened discipline, eyes glinting with a harsh expectation. Without a single word, he thrust a heavy pack into Hinadori's arms with enough force to make him stumble.

"Ten miles," Toramaru growled, his voice low and unrelenting. "Up the mountain and back. You have two hours."

Hinadori's heart sank into the pit of his stomach.

The pack felt like it was filled with lead, easily fifty pounds, and the path up the mountain was notorious for its jagged rocks and steep climbs. Even in daylight, it was treacherous. But he swallowed his frustration, knowing that any protest would fall on deaf ears. He could practically feel Toramaru's cold gaze boring into him.

With a deep breath, he secured the pack against his back and began at a jog, each step heavier than the last. The first mile was torture. His legs were still aching from the previous day's brutal training, muscles tight and unyielding as they fought to carry him forward. Every time his foot landed unevenly on the rugged terrain, the weight of the pack pulled him off balance, threatening to send him tumbling.

The mist thickened as he climbed higher, mingling with a light drizzle that soaked into his clothes, turning the rocky path into a slippery trial of endurance. His breath came in short gasps, the frigid air stinging his throat and lungs. He could feel the burn deep in his chest as if the very air were fighting him. His pace slowed, each step becoming a test of willpower.

"Keep moving, street rat!" Toramaru's voice rang out from somewhere below, sharp and cutting through the mist like a blade. "Or have you already forgotten why you're here?"

A flash of memory hit Hinadori like a hammer.

Daiki... his rival, his downfall.

The forbidden technique that had caused so much damage.

The look on Daiki's face, a mix of disbelief and agony, haunted him, fueling his shame and anger.

His fists clenched tighter around the straps of the pack. He was here to prove something, not just to Toramaru but to himself.

There was no room for weakness.

The climb felt endless, and by the time he reached the halfway point, the drizzle had turned the path into a slick and unforgiving mess. Each step became a gamble—slip, and he would crash down the mountainside. But stopping was not an option. The mountain loomed above him, indifferent to his struggle.

The descent proved even worse. His legs, worn and shaky, threatened to give out with every step. He slipped several times, his hands and knees taking the brunt of each fall as the jagged rocks bit into his skin. Blood mixed with mud, but he pushed on, refusing to let the pain slow him. He could almost hear Toramaru's mocking tone, daring him to quit.

When Hinadori finally stumbled back into the training yard, his vision blurred by sweat and exhaustion, he could barely stand. His legs gave out, sending him to his knees in the dirt. His chest heaved as he gasped for air, the pack now feeling like a mountain on his back, crushing him. His entire body shook with fatigue, every muscle screaming for relief.

But he had made it.

For a brief moment, the thought of failure left his mind.

Then, Toramaru loomed over him, his expression unreadable.

"Two hours and seventeen minutes," he said coldly. "Pathetic. Again."

Hinadori's head snapped up in disbelief. "Again? But I-"

The backhand caught him across the face, sending him sprawling.

"Did I ask for your opinion?" Toramaru snarled. "Up! Now!"

And so it went, day after day, week after week. The challenges grew more intense, more grueling. One day, Hinadori found himself standing in the icy waters of a mountain stream, holding a boulder above his head for hours on end. Another day, he was forced to spar against three of Toramaru's assistants simultaneously, his arms and legs weighted down with heavy chains.

The nights brought little respite. Often, Hinadori would be woken in the dead of night, forced to recite complex philosophical texts or solve intricate tactical puzzles. His meals, when they came, were barely enough to sustain him - cold rice, wilted vegetables, occasionally a strip of dried fish that was more bone than meat.

"You think you deserve better?" Toramaru sneered one evening, as Hinadori stared longingly at the pathetic portions that wouldn't even fill a mouse. "Prove it. Earn it."

The isolation began to take its toll. Hinadori found himself talking to the walls of his chamber, desperate for any form of interaction. He replayed memories of his time in Tuchi Market, of his conversations with Noke, clinging to them like a lifeline to sanity.

One particularly brutal day, after hours of holding excruciating poses under the scorching sun, Hinadori finally broke.

"*Why*?" he screamed at Toramaru, his voice raw with emotion. "What are you trying to prove?"

Toramaru's face darkened. He crossed the distance between them in two quick strides, grabbing Hinadori by the front of his sweat-soaked gi.

"Why?" he hissed. "Because you're weak. Because you let your emotions control you. Because you thought you could take shortcuts to power. You think being a samurai is about strength alone? It's about discipline, sacrifice, and unwavering commitment. You're not just training your body, boy. You're forging your very soul."

He released Hinadori with a shove, sending him stumbling backward.

"You want to be a samurai? Then you need to learn control, or die trying. Your lack of discipline makes you worse than useless. You're a liability, a ticking time bomb that could get your fellow samurais killed. Until you master yourself, you're nothing but a rabid dog that needs to be put down for the safety of others.

The words cut deep.

...

Later, when the sun had long since set Hinadori was preparing for another restless night.

Suddenly, a shadow fell across his door.

He looked up, startled to see the imposing figure of Saito silhouetted in the doorway.

"Grand Master Saito," Hinadori said, scrambling to his feet and bowing deeply. "I... I didn't expect..."

Saito's eyes swept over the sparse room, taking in the signs of Hinadori's isolation and grueling training. His face remained impassive, but there was a glint in his eye that Hinadori couldn't quite decipher.

"Sit," Saito commanded, gesturing to the thin mat on the floor. Hinadori complied, his heart racing.

What could Saito want with him?

Saito remained standing, looming over Hinadori like a storm cloud. "I've been watching your progress," he said, his voice low and measured. "Or should I say, your lack thereof."

Hinadori felt a flush of shame creep up his neck. "I'm trying my best, Grand Master. The training is-" Hinadori began, but was cut off by Saito's sharp, exasperated sigh.

"Excuses?" Saito cut him off, his voice sharp as a blade. "A true samurai doesn't make excuses. We fight, we endure, we die with honor if necessary. Weakness is not in the challenge, boy, but in how you face it. Pushing past your limits - that is the way of the samurai."

Hinadori's head snapped up, shock evident on his face.

A ghost of a smile played at the corners of Saito's mouth. "I knew many things, boy. Including the fact that Omo saw great potential in you." His expression hardened. "But now, I wonder if he was mistaken."

Hinadori's mind reeled. "Why bring up Omo now, of all times?" he asked.

Saito's eyes narrowed. "Because you're failing, boy. You're letting the hardships break you instead of forge you. Your mother saw a fire in you, a potential that could change the world. But all I see is a scared child, clinging to memories of the past."

Hinadori felt a surge of anger rise within him. "You don't know anything about me," he said, his voice low but intense. "Or about what I've been through."

"Don't I?" Saito raised an eyebrow. "I know more than you think, Hinadori. About your past, about Omo, about the legacy you carry without even realizing it."

Hinadori's breath caught in his throat. "What-"

Saito waved a hand dismissively. "What's important is that you're squandering the gifts you've been given. You are wallowing in self-pity."

The words stung, but they also ignited something in Hinadori.

A determination he thought he had lost.

"You're wrong," he said, staggering to his feet, one hand clutching his bruised ribs. "I haven't given up. I won't give up. Whatever potential Omo sees in me... I'll live up to it. I'll surpass it."

Saito studied him for a long moment, his expression unreadable.

Then, he turned toward the door. As he did, Hinadori called out, "Wait! Plea se... can you tell me more about my Omo?"

He paused, a flicker of something in his eyes. Then, with a grunt, he turned and strode out of the room, leaving Hinadori alone with his thoughts.

As he settled back onto his mat, Hinadori's mind raced. But even as the conversation swirled in his mind, Hinadori felt a new determination taking root. His mother had believed in him. She had left him a legacy to live up to. He wouldn't let her down.

As he drifted off to sleep, Hinadori made a silent vow. He would not only survive this training, but he would excel. He would become the samurai he had believed he could be, the warrior worthy of whatever mysterious legacy he carried.

Whatever challenges lay ahead, Hinadori was ready to face them head-on.

...

The cool morning air nipped at Hinadori's skin as he made his way to the archery range, his body still aching from the previous day's grueling exercises. As he approached, a familiar figure came into view... Archery Instructor Yumi, her long hair adorned with a single white crane feather.

"Hinadori," she called out, her voice carrying on the breeze. "Come here."

He approached cautiously, unsure of what to expect. Yumi's face was as impassive as ever, but there was something in her eyes, a softness he hadn't seen before.

"Your form has suffered," she said matter-of-factly. "Show me your draw."

Hinadori picked up a nearby bow, wincing as his injured hand protested the movement. He knocked an arrow and drew back, but the motion was clumsy, lacking its former fluidity.

Yumi clicked her tongue disapprovingly. "As I thought. Your injury has set you back considerably." She paused, studying him intently. "But perhaps... this is an opportunity."

"An opportunity, Yumi-sensei?" Hinadori asked, confusion evident in his voice.

She nodded. "To relearn. To build your skills from the ground up, free from bad habits." She took the bow from him gently. "We will start with the basics. Come, an hour before dawn each day. We will rehabilitate your form."

Hinadori felt a spark of hope ignite in his chest. "Thank you, Yumi-sensei."

And so began a new routine.

Each morning, before the sun peeked over the horizon, Hinadori would meet Yumi at the archery range. They started with simple exercises... stretching his injured hand, rebuilding its strength and flexibility.

"Patience," Yumi would remind him when frustration threatened to overwhelm him. "The bow teaches us that the path to our target is not always straight. Sometimes, we must draw back to move forward."

Slowly, painstakingly, Hinadori's skills began to return. The bow, once an awkward thing in his hands, became an extension of himself once more. But it was more than just physical rehabilitation. Yumi's calm presence and measured words were a balm to his battered spirit.

One morning, as Hinadori loosed an arrow that flew true to its mark, he felt a weight lift from his shoulders. For the first time in months, he smirked- a genuine, unguarded expression of joy.

Yumi nodded approvingly. "Good. You are finding your center."

Those words stuck with Hinadori long after the session ended.

Who was he?

The question echoed in his mind as he went through his daily training with Master Toramaru.

As he held a grueling horse stance, sweat pouring down his face, memories of his past life in Tuchi Market flooded his mind. He saw Noke's mischievous grin as they plotted their next score. He felt the warmth of Omo's hand on his shoulder, heard the old man's gentle words of wisdom.

"Focus, boy!" Toramaru's sharp voice cut through his reverie. "Your mind wanders. Control it!"

Hinadori gritted his teeth, forcing himself back to the present. But the memories lingered, like ghosts at the edges of his consciousness.

That night, as he lay on his thin sleeping mat, the doubts crept in.

Had he made the right choice in coming to the Academy?

Was this brutal training truly forging him into something better, or just breaking him down?

He thought of Noke, wondering where she was now.

Was she facing similar challenges at the Shugendo temple?

Or had she found a different path entirely?

The next day, during a particularly intense sparring session, Hinadori found himself overwhelmed by a wave of emotion. As he traded blows with one of Toramaru's assistants, he suddenly saw Omo's face instead of his opponent's. The shock of it caused him to hesitate, earning him a sharp blow to the ribs.

"Pathetic!" Toramaru barked. "What kind of samurai lets his emotions control him like that?"

Hinadori struggled to his feet, his chest heaving. "It won't happen again."

But it did happen again.

And again.

...

Memories of his past life kept intruding at the most inopportune moments, throwing him off balance, making him question everything.

One evening, as he sat in meditation, trying to clear his mind, Hinadori found himself on the verge of tears. The loneliness of his isolation, the brutality of his training, the uncertainty of his future - it all came crashing down on him at once.

"I don't know if I can do this," he whispered to the empty room. "I don't know if I'm strong enough."

But even as the words left his lips, another voice rose within him... a voice that sounded suspiciously like Noke's.

Since when has "strong enough" ever stopped us? We survived the streets, didn't we? We can survive this too.

Hinadori took a deep breath, centering himself.

Exhausted from the day's trials, Hinadori fell into a deep, dreamless sleep.

...

When he awoke, his mind was clearer than it had been since arriving at the academy. The challenges ahead no longer seemed insurmountable, but rather obstacles to be overcome.

The next morning, as he met Yumi for their archery session, she noticed a change in him.

"Your eyes are clearer today," she observed. "You've faced something within yourself."

Hinadori nodded. "I have, Yumi-sensei. I... I've been "feeling shame, doubts about everything, and experiencing flashes of my past."

Yumi was silent for a moment, then she spoke softly. "The past shapes us, Hinadori. But it does not define us. You carry the strength of your experiences with you, but you are not bound by them. Each arrow you loose is a new beginning, a chance to rewrite your story."

Her words resonated deeply with Hinadori. As he drew back the bow, he felt a new sense of purpose flooding through him. Yes, he had left his old life behind. Yes, the path ahead was difficult and uncertain. But he was not the same person who had entered the Academy all those months ago.

He was becoming something new - not by forgetting his past, but by building upon it. The street rat's cunning, Omo's wisdom, Noke's determination - all of these were part of him, shaping the samurai he was becoming.

As the arrow flew true to its mark, Hinadori felt a sense of clarity he hadn't experienced in months. The doubts were still there, lurking in the shadows of his mind. But now he had the strength to face them, to learn from them rather than be controlled by them.

He turned to Yumi, bowing deeply. "Thank you, sensei."

Yumi's lips curved in a rare smile and gave a wordless bow.

As they continued their practice, Hinadori felt a renewed sense of purpose. Whatever challenges lay ahead, he would face them head-on - not as the boy from Tuchi Market, nor as the perfect samurai the Academy sought to create, but as himself. Hinadori, with all his strengths and flaws, his past and his potential.

The path of the samurai was long and arduous, but for the first time in a long while, Hinadori felt truly ready to walk it.

...

As the weeks turned to months, Hinadori began to notice changes.

His body, once soft from street life, hardened into corded muscle. His mind, sharpened by constant challenges and sleep deprivation, became quicker, more focused. Even the verbal abuse seemed to lose its sting, rolling off him like water off a duck's back.

One morning, as Hinadori prepared for another grueling run, he caught sight of his reflection in a rain barrel. The face that stared back at him was leaner, harder, with eyes that held a steely determination. For a moment, he barely recognized himself.

"Admiring yourself?" Toramaru's mocking voice cut through his reverie. "I hope you're not getting complacent, boy. There is still much for you to learn, boy. Your journey has barely begun.."

Hinadori turned to face his tormentor - no, his teacher, he realized with a start. "No, Master Toramaru," he said, his voice steady. "I was just reflecting on how far I've come... and how far I still have to go."

Something flickered in Toramaru's eyes - *surprise? approval?* - but it was gone in an instant.

"Good," he grunted.

Chapter 8- The Next Phase

The "next phase" proved to be even more grueling than anything Hinadori had experienced before.

When he approached the training yard the next morning, he stopped short, his eyes widening in disbelief. The once-familiar space had been transformed overnight into an intricate labyrinth of obstacles and challenges. Wooden structures loomed ominously, their purposes unclear but undoubtedly demanding. The air buzzed with an almost tangible energy, as if the very atmosphere was charged with the intensity of the trials to come.

Master Toramaru stood at the entrance, his face a mask of grim determination.

"Welcome," he said, his voice carrying a weight that made Hinadori's stomach clench, "This ancient training ground has broken and remade warriors for generations. Are you ready to be forged anew?"

Hinadori swallowed hard, nodding silently as he stepped into what promised to be the most grueling phase of his journey yet.

His hands, once nimble tools for picking pockets and navigating the shadowy world of Tuchi Market, now moved with deadly precision whether wielding a sword, nocking an arrow, or striking with bare fists. His body, formerly accustomed to darting through crowded streets, had become a finely-tuned instrument of combat.

Each day brought new challenges and triumphs. In sword practice, his strikes flowed like water, each movement seamlessly connected to the next. During archery, his aim grew unerringly accurate, his breath and heartbeat synchronizing with each release of the bowstring. Even in unarmed combat, where he had once felt hopelessly outmatched, Hinadori now moved with a fluid grace that often caught his opponents off-guard.

But it wasn't just his physical skills that had improved. Hinadori's mind had sharpened too, honed by endless tactical exercises and meditation sessions. He could now read an opponent's intentions in the subtlest shift of their stance, anticipating attacks before they even began.

Then, one frosty morning, came a new test. Hinadori stood in the center of the yard, a thick blindfold obscuring his vision. The chill air nipped at his exposed skin, and he could hear his own steady breathing in the darkness. Every sense seemed heightened... the rustle of leaves, the crunch of gravel underfoot, the faint metallic clink of armor... each sound painting a picture in his mind's eye.

"*Hajimeru*," Toramaru's voice echoed through the cold morning, setting the first obstacle in motion.

Hinadori stepped forward cautiously, his arms stretched out in front of him. The ground beneath his feet was uneven, dotted with hidden pitfalls and loose stones. He stumbled, catching himself just before a sharp-edged rock would have sliced his shin. From somewhere ahead, he heard the soft creak of wooden beams—a trap.

His body tensed. Relying solely on his hearing and sense of touch, he moved carefully, anticipating the next obstacle. The wind shifted, carrying with it the subtle groan of ropes under tension. A swinging log, he realized too late, and it was upon him. He ducked, narrowly avoiding the strike as it whooshed past his ear, the force strong enough to knock him flat had it connected.

Blindfolded or not, Hinadori knew this new training ground had been remade into a death trap. Spiked posts, swinging weights, shallow pits filled with icy water—each misstep could send him crashing into one. His heart hammered, but he moved with increasing confidence, feeling the cold dirt beneath his feet, listening for subtle changes in the environment. A wooden post whizzed past his shoulder, and Hinadori spun away, brushing against its rough surface but staying upright.

After what felt like hours of blind fumbling, the blindfold was ripped off. The cold sting of daylight was a strange comfort as his vision cleared, but no reprieve was granted. A new phase began immediately.

He lowered himself chest-deep into the icy water, shivering uncontrollably as the bitter cold sank into his bones. His limbs were leaden, his breath shallow. Toramaru ordered him to submerge, and Hinadori forced himself under the water, the shock making him gasp before he held his breath. The water seemed to freeze his muscles in place as he pushed through the pain, emerging again only when Toramaru's count reached the prescribed number. Each time, the count grew longer, and Hinadori's body trembled violently as he fought to control his breathing. The cold assaulted his senses, but every time he surfaced, Toramaru's stern expression drove him to keep going.

But the icy water was just the beginning.

As Hinadori stumbled out of the stream, his limbs numb and shaking, he found himself facing a gauntlet of challenges. There were scalding hot coals to walk across, testing his focus and pain tolerance. Massive logs swung from ropes, threatening to knock him off narrow balance beams. In one corner, a pit of mud awaited, where he would grapple with other trainees, each trying to subdue the other in the slippery mire. Every task seemed designed to push him to his absolute limits and beyond.

"Faster!" Toramaru's voice cut through the clatter of weapons as Hinadori found himself once again in the sparring ring, surrounded by multiple opponents. Their wooden swords slashed through the air, the sharp whoosh filling his ears as they aimed for him without mercy. "React, don't think! Let your body move on its own!"

Hinadori's muscles screamed in protest, still stiff from the icy water, but he forced himself into action. He ducked beneath a swinging sword, rolled to avoid another strike, then shot up into a defensive stance. His wooden sword snapped upward to parry a blow aimed at his head, and without hesitation, he pivoted to deflect another strike coming from his right. His breathing was labored, but his movements became smoother, more precise with each passing moment.

Where once Hinadori had fought with wild desperation, relying on brute strength and the luck of survival, now he was adapting. He could sense the rhythm of his opponents, the subtle shifts in their stance, the way their muscles tensed just before a strike. He flowed around them, moving like water, countering with grace rather than force. His body began to anticipate their moves before his mind could, instinct guiding him in the brutal dance of survival.

Hours passed in a blur of pain and exertion, but Toramaru wasn't finished. When the sparring finally ceased, and his body was ready to collapse, the true challenge began.

That evening, Toramaru led him to the meditation room, where Hinadori knelt in seiza, legs tucked beneath him, his back straight despite the bone-deep exhaustion that ached through every muscle. His legs soon became numb, but he forced himself to remain still as the weight of the day's training pressed down on him. He was ready to face anything physical, but the mental test that came next unnerved him in ways he hadn't expected.

Toramaru's voice, low and deliberate, broke the silence. "You're in a village," he began, his tone cold and precise. "A group of bandits is in the midst of their raid. They've already killed several villagers and are terrorizing the rest, stealing everything of value. You can save the remaining villagers, but only by sacrificing an innocent child. Keep in mind that this child is the son of the village elder, one of the people you'd be saving. What do you do?"

Hinadori's heart skipped a beat. His mind raced through the possibilities, searching for a way out, but the weight of the dilemma hung over him. He had always trained to save lives, to protect the weak, but the scenario Toramaru posed left no room for easy answers. The burden of the decision pressed down on his shoulders, made heavier by the personal element introduced.

How could he look the village elder in the eye after sacrificing their child?

But how could he condemn an entire village to save one life, no matter how innocent?

He felt the burden of the decision, its gravity pressing down on his shoulders.

"I..." he started hesitantly, his voice shaking. "I would try to find another way. To save both the villagers and the child."

Toramaru's eyes narrowed, his gaze sharp as a blade. "And if there is no other way?" His voice was unyielding. "If it's one life against many?"

Hinadori hesitated, feeling the cold grip of reality tighten around him. He knew what Toramaru expected, what the answer would be. With a deep breath, he forced the words out. "Then... would sacrifice myself," Hinadori said, his voice steady. "No innocent life is worth losing, especially not a child's. If my death could save the village, that's a price I'm willing to pay."

For a long moment, Toramaru was silent. Then, he nodded slowly, approval hidden behind his stern expression. "Good," he said, his voice softer now. "A samurai must be prepared to make impossible choices, to bear burdens that would break lesser men. Remember this lesson well, Hinadori. These decisions will shape you."

Hinadori's mind reeled as he bowed his head, the weight of the training settling deep into his bones. The lessons, both physical and moral, were harsh, but they were forging him into something stronger, something sharper. Yet, the path ahead felt heavier with each step he took.

...

As the seasons changed, Hinadori found himself changing too. The anger and resentment that had fueled him in the beginning gave way to a calm determination. The isolation, once maddening, became a source of strength, forcing him to look inward, to confront his own weaknesses and fears.

One night, as he lay on his thin sleeping mat, staring at the ceiling, Hinadori realized something profound. The path of the samurai wasn't just about physical prowess or martial skill. It was about forging oneself into a weapon of justice, a shield for the innocent. It was about transcending one's own limitations and becoming something greater.

The next morning, as he stood before Toramaru, ready for another day of grueling training,

Hinadori felt... different.

Centered.

Focused.

Ready.

Toramaru studied him for a long moment, his expression unreadable.

Then, to Hinadori's shock, the master grunted in approval.

"You've come far, Hinadori," he said, his voice gruff but tinged with something that might have been respect. "But your journey is far from over. Are you prepared for what comes next?"

Hinadori bowed, deep and respectful. "Yes, Master Toramaru," he said, his voice steady and sure. "I am ready for whatever challenges lie ahead."

As they moved to the training yard, Hinadori caught a glimpse of other students in the distance. For the first time in months, he felt a flicker of connection to the outside world. But he pushed the feeling aside, focusing on the task at hand. His isolation might be coming to an end, but the true test of his growth was yet to come.

Whatever lay ahead, Hinadori knew one thing for certain: he was no longer the impulsive, angry boy who had used a forbidden technique in a moment of desperation. He had been broken down and rebuilt, forged in the fires of Toramaru's relentless training.

As Hinadori stood there, ready to face whatever challenges lay ahead, he realized that the samurai he once dreamed of becoming was no longer just a distant ideal. It was taking form within him, shaped by every hardship and trial he'd endured. The pain that once threatened to break him now fueled his transformation. His body craved the forge of adversity, knowing that each challenge would only make him stronger. Hinadori was no longer just a student of the Bushido Academy; he was becoming the embodiment of its teachings, ready to face whatever trials awaited him next.

Chapter 9– The Dagger's Significance

The mournful hooting of owls pierced the veil of Hinadori's fitful sleep.

His eyes snapped open, body tensing instinctively for the harsh wake-up call that had become routine in his isolated training. But the expected shout never came. The silence stretched on, broken only by the gentle rustling of leaves outside his window.

Hinadori sat up slowly, confusion furrowing his brow. The pale light of the waning moon filtered through the paper screens, casting elongated shadows across the sparse room. He glanced at the water clock in the corner, it was the dead of night, the hour when he was usually dragged from his bed for grueling exercises.

But tonight, all was still.

Curiosity overtook caution. Hinadori rose quietly, wincing as his muscles protested the movement. He reached for his *haori*, a light jacket worn over his sleeping *yukata*. The nights had grown colder, autumn's chill settling over the academy like a heavy blanket.

Sliding the door open with practiced stealth, Hinadori peered into the darkened hallway. No sign of Master Toramaru or any of the other instructors. Taking a deep breath, he stepped out into the night.

The academy grounds were transformed in the moonlight. Familiar buildings took on an ethereal quality, their edges softened by shadow. Hinadori moved cautiously, his bare feet silent on the worn stone paths.

He passed the archery range first, the targets looming like silent sentinels in the darkness. Memories of his sessions with Yumi-sensei flickered through his mind... the patient guidance, the gradual rebuilding of his skills. For a moment, Hinadori was tempted to slip inside, to feel the comforting weight of a bow in his hands. But he pressed on, drawn by some inexplicable urge to explore further.

The next landmark he encountered was the meditation garden. By day, it was a place of serene beauty, carefully raked gravel swirling around islands of moss and stone. Now, in the half-light, it seemed almost alive. The patterns in the gravel shifted and danced, creating the illusion of rippling water. Hinadori paused, mesmerized by the play of shadow and moonlight.

A soft sound broke his reverie... a tiny mew, barely audible. Hinadori turned, searching for the source. There, huddled beneath a gnarled pine, was a small kitten. Its fur was a patchwork of orange and white, eyes gleaming like liquid gold in the darkness.

"Hello there, little one," Hinadori whispered, crouching down. He extended a hand slowly, not wanting to startle the creature. The kitten regarded him warily for a moment before inching closer, curiosity overcoming caution.

As Hinadori's fingers brushed its soft fur, the kitten playfully batted at his sleeve. Its tiny claws caught in the fabric, tugging insistently. There was a small popping sound, and Hinadori watched in dismay as one of the toggles fastening his *haori* came loose, bouncing across the gravel.

The kitten, delighted by this new toy, pounced after it.

"Wait!" Hinadori hissed, scrambling to his feet. But the nimble creature was already darting away, the toggle clutched triumphantly in its mouth.

With a resigned sigh, Hinadori gave chase. The kitten led him on a merry dance through the moonlit grounds, always staying just out of reach. They wove between buildings, skirted training areas, and ducked through overgrown gardens rarely visited by students.

Finally, breathless and slightly disoriented, Hinadori found himself in a part of the academy he'd never seen before. The buildings here were older, their wood darkened with age. Moss crept up the walls, and the air held a musty scent of secrets long kept.

The kitten darted around a corner, and Hinadori followed... only to pull up short, his heart leaping into his throat. There, not ten paces away, was a door unlike any he'd seen in the academy. It was massive, easily twice his height, carved from a single piece of dark wood. Intricate patterns swirled across its surface, depicting scenes of battle and mystical creatures that seemed to shift and move in the moonlight.

Hinadori knew, with a certainty that chilled him to his core, that this must be the back entrance to the Chamber, the secret heart of the Bushido Academy, where the masters convened to shape the fates of students and samurai alike.

As if summoned by his realization, voices drifted from beyond the door. Hinadori's eyes widened in panic. He looked around frantically for a hiding place, spotting a deep shadow cast by a nearby pillar. He dove for cover just as the massive door began to swing open.

Hinadori pressed himself against the rough wood of the pillar, hardly daring to breathe. The kitten, apparently sensing his distress, had gone still in his arms. Together, they watched as the Chamber masters filed out into the space.

Grand Master Saito led the procession, his face set in grim lines. Behind him came the other masters Hinadori recognized - Toramaru, Ryugen, Tsuruko, and Kumayama. But there were others too, figures shrouded in shadows, their features indistinct.

"Are you certain of this information, Saito?" one of the shadow-figures asked, its voice a sibilant whisper.

Saito nodded gravely. "My sources are reliable. The dagger was indeed in the possession of the girl, Nokemono."

Hinadori's breath caught in his throat. Noke? What did she have to do with this?

"And you're sure it's the true artifact?" This from Master Ryugen, his golden eyes gleaming in the darkness. "Not some clever forgery?"

"I've seen it with my own eyes," Saito confirmed. "It bears all the markings described in the ancient texts. There can be no doubt, it is the companion blade to the *Shi no Kaze.*"

A collective murmur ran through the assembled masters. Hinadori strained to catch every word, his mind reeling. The Wind of Death... he remembered that night on the bridge, the awesome and terrifying power that had emanated from the blade Saito wielded.

But a companion Shi No Kaze?

And Noke had it?

Hinadori's mind reeled at the implications. If the Wind of Death was already a weapon of unimaginable power, what could its companion be capable of? And how did it relate to Noke? The pieces of a larger puzzle were slowly coming together, but the full picture remained frustratingly out of reach.

Master Tsuruko spoke next, her melodious voice tinged with concern. "If this is true, then the girl's importance cannot be overstated. Even though we now possess the *Shi no Ibuki*, the Breath of Mortality, she must be brought into the fold, trained to understand its power. Her connection to it could be crucial."

"Bah!" Master Kumayama's growl cut through the night. "We have the dagger now. Why bother with the street urchin at all?"

"Because power like this isn't just about possession," Saito's voice was sharp. "The girl's innate connection to the dagger could be key to unlocking its full potential. No, we must proceed carefully. The Shi no kaze and *Shi no ibuki* are not mere weapons to be wielded by untrained hands, even our own."

One of the shadow-figures stepped forward, its form seeming to ripple and shift. "Perhaps it is time we shared the full history with the council, Saito. If we are to make informed decisions about both the dagger and the girl, we must know all."

Saito was silent for a long moment, his hand unconsciously moving to touch the concealed dagger at his side. Then he nodded. "Very well. Listen closely, for this tale has been passed down through generations of the Chamber, known only to a select few."

Hinadori held his breath, every fiber of his being focused on Saito's words.

"Long ago, before the Great War that nearly tore our realm asunder, the Emperor commissioned a masterful swordsmith to create a set of five elemental swords and a safeguard sword to complete the set. The safeguard sword was meant to be the most powerful of all. He feared the possibility of his own warriors turning against the throne, and sought a weapon that could quell any rebellion."

"The result was the *Shi No Kaze* - a blade of unparalleled power, capable of cutting through not just flesh and bone, but the very fabric of reality itself. But such power came at a terrible cost. The sword's wielder risked being consumed by its hunger for destruction and revenge.

"Recognizing this danger, the swordsmith's son later forged a companion blade - the dagger now in Nokemono's possession. This dagger was designed to amplify the Wind of Death's power while also protecting its wielder from the sword's devastating effects. Together, they formed a perfect balance of destruction and protection. The swordsmith's son forged Shi no Ibuki not just as a companion blade, but to make *Shi No Kaze* the most feared sword for destruction and revenge, a tribute to his father's unparalleled skill.

Master Ryugen's voice was hushed with awe. "The elemental blades of legend... I had thought them mere myth."

Saito shook his head. "No myth, old friend. *Shi No Kaze* and *Shi no Ibuki* are part of a set of five elemental blades - Wind, Earth, Fire, Water, and Lightning. Each possesses unique properties, tied to the fundamental forces of nature."

"And the girl's father..." Tsuruko began, her voice trailing off.

"Yes," Saito confirmed. "Nokemono's father was known as the legend who helped found the House of Blood. He brought together the wielders of these mystical blades, uniting them in service to the Emperor. There are six blades in total, each imbued with incredible power. But the Wind of Death... it stands above the rest, for as we all know, death comes for us all in the end."

A heavy silence fell over the gathered masters. Hinadori's mind was spinning, trying to process the enormity of what he was hearing. Noke's dagger was part of an ancient set of magical weapons? Her father had been some kind of legendary warrior?

"There's more," Saito continued, his voice dropping even lower. "The creation of these blades is tied to an even greater conflict - an epic battle between good and evil, when an ancient darkness tried to consume our world. The details have been scattered throughout the land and lost to time, but the power contained in these weapons... it's a remnant of that primordial struggle."

Master Kumayama snorted derisively. "Pretty stories, Saito. But what does this have to do with our present situation? With the boy?"

Hinadori's heart skipped a beat.

Were they talking about him?

Saito's eyes seemed to gleam in the darkness. "Everything, my old friend. Hinadori's presence here, his connection to Nokemono... it's not mere coincidence. They are both part of a larger destiny, one that even I do not fully understand."

"You speak in riddles, Saito," Toramaru growled. "If the boy is so important, why subject him to such brutal training?"

"Because he must be ready," Saito replied, his voice firm. "Whatever role he is to play, whatever challenges lie ahead, Hinadori must be forged into a weapon as keen as the blades we speak of. His potential is vast, but untapped. We must push him to his limits and beyond."

"And the girl?" Tsuruko asked. "What of her training at the Shugendo temple?"

Saito shook his head. "That remains a mystery. Our contacts within the temple have been... unreliable of late. But I fear time grows short. We must-"

A sudden movement caught Hinadori's eye. The kitten, which had been remarkably still throughout the conversation, chose that moment to wriggle free from his grasp. With a soft mew, it darted out from behind the pillar, streaking across the moonlit courtyard.

"What was that?" Kumayama's voice boomed. "There! A shadow by the pillar!"

Hinadori's heart threatened to burst from his chest. He pressed himself flat against the wood, willing himself to become one with the shadows. He heard the sound of footsteps approaching, saw the flicker of a lantern's light.

"Probably just a stray cat," Tsuruko's voice came, mercifully close. "See? There are its prints in the dust."

"Hmph," Kumayama grumbled. "I still say we should check-"

"Enough," Saito's commanding tone cut through the night. "We've lingered here too long. Let us return to the Chamber and discuss our next moves."

The footsteps receded, and Hinadori heard the creak of the massive door swinging shut. Only when the last echo had faded did he dare to move, his legs trembling as he slid down the pillar to sit on the cool stone.

His mind was a whirlwind of questions and revelations.

Noke, the dagger, the Wind of Death, the House of Blood... and somehow, he was connected to it all?

It seemed impossible, like something out of the fantastical stories Omo used to tell on cold winter nights.

But Hinadori knew what he had heard. And more importantly, he knew that his path - already difficult and uncertain - had just become infinitely more complex.

As the first hints of dawn began to lighten the eastern sky, Hinadori made his way back to his quarters. His body moved on autopilot, his mind still reeling from the night's discoveries. He had much to ponder, and precious little time before his grueling training would resume.

But one thing was certain... nothing would ever be the same again.

Chapter 10- Tides of Adversity

H inadori had barely closed his eyes when a sharp knock startled him awake.

Yuki's stern voice came through the door, "Hinadori-san, get up. You're needed."

Still groggy, he rubbed his eyes and slid the door open, squinting against the early morning light that filtered into his small room. Yuki stood in the doorway, her face as unreadable as ever, her dark eyes giving nothing away.

"You've earned your place back with the other trainees," she said flatly. "Go to the center courtyard now."

Without waiting for a response, Yuki turned on her heel and left, her footsteps fading down the hall. Hinadori remained in the doorway for a moment, watching her go, feeling a strange mixture of relief and dread.

He closed the door and paced the cramped room, his thoughts swirling in a chaotic mess. The events of the previous night replayed in his mind, each revelation weighing heavier than the last- the *Shi No Kaze*, Noke's involvement, and his own mysterious destiny.

How could he face everyone with all this secret knowledge?

And then there was the fight with Daiki. The memory of that forbidden technique made his stomach churn.

Hinadori took a deep breath, remembering Yumi-sensei's lessons. He'd been through too much to back down now. With that thought, he stepped outside and started walking. The early morning air was crisp, the sky just beginning to lighten with the soft hues of dawn.

He made his footsteps steady and sure.

The center courtyard seemed vast, almost overwhelming after months spent in isolation. As Hinadori entered, he felt the weight of every gaze turn toward him. The other trainees were quick to react, snickers and hushed whispers spreading like wildfire.

"Look who's back," Daiki muttered under his breath, his lips curling into a sneer. "Thought you'd be too scared to show your face."

Hano, standing just a few steps away, cracked his knuckles loudly. "Bet he's forgotten how to fight," he said with a smirk. "He won't last a minute out here."

Rin simply watched him with those sharp, calculating eyes. She didn't say anything, but Hinadori could feel her sizing him up, weighing his every step.

For a moment, the old Hinadori, the one who would've slunk away in shame, overwhelmed by their mockery, almost resurfaced.

But this time was different.

He had changed.

Where their scorn might have once made him shrink, now he held his head high, shoulders squared. Their words barely registered.

"You have something to say, Daiki?" Hinadori asked, his voice calm, but with an edge that caught the others off guard.

Daiki's sneer faltered, but only for a moment. "Just surprised you showed up, that's all," he said, louder now, trying to regain control of the conversation. "Must have gotten soft in isolation."

Hinadori stopped, turning slightly to face him. "Maybe," he said evenly, his eyes locking onto Daiki's, "but soft or not, I'm still standing here. That's more than you can say for someone who couldn't land a clean hit last time."

A few trainees exchanged surprised looks, a couple even stifling laughs. Daiki's face darkened, but before he could respond, Master Kaito stepped forward, his voice sharp.

"Trainees," he said.

At that, everyone turned to see not only Master Kaito approaching, but the other trainers as well. Hinadori blinked, amazed by the strong presence of the three of them, which felt powerful even from a distance. Master Swordsman Kaito, with his lean body, looked ready to move at any moment. His sharp eyes scanned the students like a predator watching its prey. Next to him, Archery Instructor Yumi walked calm and poised, her robes barely moving in the soft breeze. Her peaceful attitude was completely different from Akio, the Hand-to-Hand Combat Specialist, who looked wild and ready for a fight, his stance full of energy.

"Listen well, for what I'm about to say will shape your destinies." Master Kaito announced, his gaze sweeping over the assembled trainees. "Over the next few days, you will face a series of tests, not just of your physical prowess, but of your mental and spiritual fortitude."

A curious murmur spread across the trainees, but it ended abruptly when Master Kaito clicked his tongue.

He continued, "These trials will determine which of you will represent the Bushido Academy at the upcoming tournament with the Shugendo Temple. Only the most worthy among you will earn that honor."

Hinadori almost choked when he heard the words.

The Shugendo Temple.

Noke.

For a while, the master seemed to continue speaking without words. Hinadori watched as Master Kaito's mouth opened and closed, but he could only hear his own thoughts.

If I could secure a spot in the tournament, I might see her again.

The thought shot through him like a bolt of electricity, fueling a fierce determination deep within. He not only missed her, but also felt a strong urge to share what he had learned the night before.

This tournament would be his chance to do just that.

"Now," Master Kaito announced, his words like sharpened steel as Hinadori was once again able to focus on them. "First, you'll face Master Yumi's test of focus."

She stepped forward, her crane feather swaying gently.

"You'll stand waist-deep in ice-cold mountain streams," she explained, her soft voice belying the challenge ahead. "While maintaining your balance on slippery rocks, you must hit moving targets with your arrows. The frigid water will numb your body, the current will fight your every move, and the mist will obscure your vision. Your mind must become an unwavering flame in a storm."

But where once these looks might have made him falter, Hinadori now felt a new strength within him. He lifted his chin, squaring his shoulders, and turned his attention back to the masters.

Master Akio's gravelly voice drew attention next. "In my trial, you'll enter the Cave of Desolation," he growled, a wicked gleam in his eye. "Ancient magics will pull the darkest fears from your minds, giving them form. Shadowy apparitions of your failures, your doubts, your shameful secrets – all will confront you. You must fight these phantoms, not just with your fists, but with the strength of your convictions."

Master Toramaru's massive frame blocked out the sun as he spoke. "But that's not all." His lips curled into a cruel smile. "The true test of your mettle lies ahead in the Crucible of Unity."

Master Ryugen stepped forward, his golden eyes seeming to peer into their very souls. "This trial will push you beyond your individual limits and force you to work as one," he intoned, his voice carrying the weight of ages.

Master Yumi's serene voice cut through the tension. "The Crucible of Unity is not just a test of skill, but of spirit and cooperation," she explained, her eyes sweeping over the gathered trainees. "You will enter a shared mindscape, each in your own realm shaped by your deepest fears and greatest strengths."

Toramaru proclaimed with authority, "Within this mental landscape, you'll face challenges that can only be overcome by working together, even as you remain physically separated."

Yumi's voice softened. "Remember, what you experience will feel real. The dangers, the triumphs, the failures - all will leave their mark on your spirit. Choose wisely, act with purpose, and above all, never lose sight of who you are and why you fight."

A bead of sweat rolled down Hinadori's temple. Yet, his mind was clear, free from the hesitation that once plagued him. The months of isolation had honed his focus, allowing him to face these challenges with a newfound sense of calm determination.

As the masters concluded their explanations, a heavy stillness settled over the courtyard, like a thick fog.

Taking a deep breath, he centered himself, recalling Yumi's teachings. He continued to show calmness and ease without emotion. The air felt cool and refreshing as he inhaled, grounding him for the trials ahead. He felt a pulse of resolve building within, ready to confront whatever lay in store.

As the masters walked away, an uncomfortable silence settled over the trainees. Hinadori stood apart, acutely aware of the gulf between him and the others. Daiki stepped forward, a sneer forming on his lips.

"Now, where were we-" Daiki began, but Rin cut him off.

"Save your breath, Daiki," she said sharply. "We've got bigger concerns than your petty rivalries." She turned to address the group, her eyes flickering briefly to Hinadori. "These trials sound like they'll test more than just our skills. We'll need to be prepared for anything."

Hano grunted, crossing his massive arms. "Bah, all this talk of *mental fortitude* and *spiritual strength*. Give me a good fight any day."

"That attitude might be why you're struggling, Hano," Rin retorted coolly.

Hinadori blinked, surprised to be included, even tangentially, in the conversation. He opened his mouth to speak, but hesitated, unsure of his place.

Daiki scoffed, tossing a dismissive glance at Hinadori. "Come on, let's go. We've got preparation to do, and I'd rather not waste any more time here."

As the group turned to leave, Hinadori caught Rin giving him a last, appraising look before she followed the others. Left alone in the courtyard, Hinadori paused for a moment to take in everything that had happened before returning to his own quarters.

...

That night, Hinadori tossed and turned on his thin sleeping mat. No matter what he tried, sleep would not come. His mind was too full of thoughts of the upcoming trials.

A fire ignited in his gut. He *has* to pass these tests, *has* to make it to the tournament.

Sleep eluded him as he visualized standing in the icy mountain stream, trying to maintain his focus while firing arrows.

Suddenly, Hinadori sat bolt upright, his eyes wide in the darkness. "I need to prepare," he whispered to himself, the realization hitting him like a splash of cold water.

Before he could talk himself out of it, Hinadori was on his feet, pulling on his clothes. He crept through the silent halls like a shadow, old habits from Tuchi Market serving him well.

The night air bit at his skin as he made his way across the Academy grounds. He moved with purpose, heading towards a small stream that ran near the edge of the property. It was a poor substitute for a raging mountain torrent, but it would have to do. Hinadori stood at the bank, staring at the inky water.

"This is stupid," he whispered, even as he started stripping down. "Absolutely insane."

The water looked black in the moonlight, and he could already feel the chill emanating from its surface. But he didn't hesitate. With gritted teeth, he waded in. The first step into the stream nearly made him yelp. The shock of the cold water nearly took his breath away. It was like knives stabbing into his foot, his leg, his waist as he waded deeper.

Hinadori gasped, his body instinctively wanting to retreat.

But he forced himself to go deeper, until the water reached his waist.

His skin prickled with goosebumps, and he could feel his muscles tensing against the chill.

Hinadori hissed through clenched teeth. His body screamed at him to get out, to run back to his warm bed.

Just as he was about to give up, a memory surfaced. Omo's weathered face, his kind eyes. "The mind controls the body, boy," the old man's voice echoed in his head. "Not the other way around."

So, he planted his feet on the slippery rocks and forced himself to stand still. Hinadori closed his eyes and focused on his breathing, just as Yumi had taught him. He imagined drawing his bow, feeling the tension in the string, visualizing the perfect shot.

Hours seemed to pass as Hinadori stood there, sometimes completely still, other times practicing his drawing motion. The cold became a constant, dull ache, but he pushed through it, training his mind to focus despite the discomfort. Hinadori's teeth chattered, his muscles ached, but he stayed put.

When he finally stumbled out of the stream, the sky was turning gray with dawn. Hinadori's fingers were numb as he pulled on his clothes but there was a fire of determination burning in his chest. He had taken the first step in preparing himself for the trials ahead.

Sneaking back to his quarters, wet and shivering but oddly invigorated, Hinadori felt a new confidence growing within him. He may not have the advantages of noble birth or years of formal training, but he had something just as powerful: the will to push himself beyond his limits.

"Bring it on, Master Yumi," he muttered, heading back to his room. He had a long day ahead, but for the first time since the trials were announced, Hinadori felt ready to face them.

As he finally lay down to catch a few hours of sleep before the official training began, Hinadori allowed himself a small, satisfied smile.

...

The sun had barely crested the horizon when Hinadori and the other trainees gathered at the base of a mist-shrouded mountain. The air was crisp, carrying the scent of pine and the distant rumble of rushing water. Yumi stood before them, her usual serene expression replaced by one of stern determination.

"Follow me," she said simply, turning to lead them up a winding path.

As they climbed, Hinadori felt the others watching him. Daiki's gaze burned with resentment, while Rin's eyes held a hint of curiosity. Hano just grunted, already breathing heavily from the ascent.

The path ended abruptly at the edge of a roaring river. The water, fed by melting snow, was a frothing mass of white foam and sharp rocks. Master Yumi gestured to a series of wooden platforms stretching out over the rapids.

Master Yumi gestured to a series of stone platforms jutting out from the river-bank, partially submerged in the rushing water.

"This is where you'll prove your focus," she announced. "You'll stand on these platforms, waist-deep in the river. Your task is to hit the targets I release upstream. They'll be moving fast, so stay sharp."

Hinadori's heart raced, but he felt a surge of confidence. His late-night training session might just pay off.

As they waded into the frigid water, curses and gasps echoed off the canyon walls. Daiki's face went pale, his teeth chattering audibly. Rin managed to keep her composure, but her knuckles were white as she gripped her bow. Even Hano's bravado faltered as the icy current tugged at his massive frame.

Hinadori sucked in a sharp breath as the water reached his waist, but he forced himself to breathe steadily, just as he'd practiced. He planted his feet on the slippery platform, finding his balance. The bite of cold water was an old friend now, familiar from countless dawn sessions during his isolation. His body, forged in Toramaru's crucible, welcomed the challenge.

"Begin!" Yumi's voice rang out, and the first targets came hurtling downstream.

The first volley was chaos.

Arrows zipped past wildly, splashing into the river or ricocheting off nearby rocks with hollow clangs. Hano, relying on his brute strength, tried to fight against the current. His foot slipped on the slick stones, and with a thunderous splash, he toppled into the rushing water.

Hinadori watched, learning from Hano's mistake.

He adjusted his stance, moving with the river rather than against it. His first arrow sailed wide, but he didn't flinch. Instead, he read the river's current and the target's speed, releasing his second arrow with precision.

Thunk!

The arrow buried itself in the dead center of the target.

The training area stilled for a moment. The other trainees murmured, surprised. Rin's eyes narrowed in on him, her usual calm replaced with a mix of curiosity and competitive fire.

As the challenge intensified, Hinadori found himself torn. Part of him wanted to offer advice to his struggling peers, but another part knew this was a competition. Each successful shot brought him closer to the tournament, closer to Noke.

Daiki's frustration morphed into grit as he fought through his discomfort, his noble pride propelling him forward.

Slowly, his aim sharpened, and his arrows started to hit more consistently. Rin, ever analytical, adapted quickly, her arrows landing true with cool, calculated precision.

Hano, however, was still struggling after his fall.

"This is impossible!" he bellowed after missing his tenth shot in a row.

Hinadori hesitated, then called out, "The river is not your opponent to be conquered, but a teacher to be understood. Flow with its current, become one with its rhythm."

Hano's head snapped around, surprise replacing anger on his face. After a moment's hesitation, he gave a curt nod and adjusted his stance.

The grueling test stretched on, each trainee pushing themselves to outdo the others. Hinadori felt his strength building with each passing moment, his body humming with energy as if the freezing water was feeding his spirit rather than sapping it. He had found his flow, each target seeming to slow in his vision as his arrows found their mark.

Yumi called out, "Final round! These targets are smaller and faster. Land a hit, and you pass. Miss, and all your previous efforts are for naught."

The tension was palpable as five tiny targets came rushing downstream, weaving erratically through the white water. Fear flickered across each trainee's face, quickly masked by determination.

Daiki's arrow veered wildly off course, and his curse was loud enough to cut through the roar of the water. Rin's arrow skimmed her target, but it didn't stick. Hano, having taken Hinadori's advice to heart, managed to clip the edge of his target.

Hinadori steadied himself, pushing thoughts of Noke and his past to the back of his mind. He focused solely on the present moment, on the bow in his hands and the target ahead. Time slowed, and the sound of the river seemed to separate into individual drops. He nocked an arrow and drew it back, muscles coiling like a spring. There was a brief, perfect pause between breaths, and he let the arrow fly.

It shot through the air with deadly accuracy, burying itself in the center of the target. The satisfying thunk echoed through the silence that followed.

"Enough," Yumi's voice cut through the silence. "Return to shore. We have seen what we needed to see."

As the trainees waded back through the icy water, their clothes heavy and dripping, Yumi's eyes lingered on Hinadori with an unreadable expression. They had all been humbled by the river, their perceived strengths tested and found wanting.

Rin caught Hinadori's eye.

"Not bad," she said, her voice cool as ever, but there was a flicker of respect in her gaze. "Though I'm curious where a street rat learned such focus."

Hano lumbered past, his heavy steps splashing through the shallows. He gave Hinadori a curt nod. "Thanks for the tip," he muttered, barely louder than the river's constant rush.

Daiki, on the other hand, refused to even glance at Hinadori. His jaw clenched tight, his face twisted in frustration, wounded pride written in every line of his body.

As they made their way back to the academy, Hinadori's thoughts returned to Noke and the challenges that still lay ahead. He had passed this test, but he knew the true trials were only beginning.

Chapter 12 - Echoes of Fear

The moon hung low in the sky, casting long shadows across Hinadori's small room. The Cave of Desolation loomed in his mind, a yawning maw of darkness ready to swallow him whole.

"Ancient magics will pull the darkest fears from your minds, giving them form," Master Akio had said. *"Shadowy apparitions of your failures, your doubts, your shameful secrets... all will confront you"*

He lay on his back, staring at the ceiling, sleep eluding him once again.

"What am I afraid of?" he whispered to the empty room.

Hinadori sat up, running a hand through his tangled hair. He needed to prepare, to steel himself against whatever horrors the cave might conjure. But how does one prepare for their own fears?

He stood, pacing the narrow confines of his quarters. His bare feet made soft padding sounds on the worn tatami mats.

"Loneliness," he muttered, ticking off a finger. "I'm afraid of being alone, of losing everyone."

But how would that take shape?

It didn't seem right. Hinadori shook his head, unsettled by the thought, yet still unsatisfied.

He moved to the small writing desk in the corner, lighting a candle with trembling hands. The flame flickered, casting dancing shadows on the walls. Hinadori grabbed a brush and began to write, his strokes quick and messy.

"Losing control," he wrote, remembering the incident with the forbidden technique. A chill ran down his spine at the memory.

But again... *how would he fight such a fear?* He couldn't very well punch his own lack of control.

Frustrated, Hinadori crumpled the paper and tossed it aside. He resumed his pacing, this time with more intensity.

"Abandonment," he said aloud, his voice barely a whisper. Images flashed through his mind - his parents, long gone; Omo, lost to the cruelty of the streets; Noke, following her own path. The ache in his chest was almost physical. Images of Akari's lifeless body flashed through his mind, the weight of his failure to protect her crushing his spirit anew. The guilt of her death still haunted him, a constant reminder of his past weaknesses.

Hinadori stopped at the small window, gazing out at the moonlit academy grounds. He pressed his forehead against the cool wood of the frame, trying to calm his racing thoughts.

"What else?" he murmured, wracking his brain. "What am I truly afraid of?"

He turned back to the room, his eyes falling on his training sword propped in the corner. Hinadori picked it up, feeling its familiar weight in his hands. He began to move through basic forms, hoping the repetitive motions might clear his mind.

As he flowed from one stance to the next, a new thought struck him. "Not living up to my potential," he said, his voice stronger now. "Disappointing those who believe in me."

The sword whistled through the air as Hinadori increased the speed of his movements. Sweat beaded on his brow, but he pushed on, his muscles burning with exertion.

"But how do I fight that?" he panted, finishing the sequence with a final, decisive strike. "How do I prove to myself that I'm worthy?"

Hinadori lowered the sword, his chest heaving. He had no answers, only more questions. The night was slipping away, and he felt no more prepared than when he'd started.

With a sigh, he returned the sword to its place and slumped down onto his sleeping mat. He closed his eyes, trying to center himself as Yumi had taught him. But inner peace remained elusive.

"Maybe that's the point," Hinadori mused, opening his eyes to stare at the ceiling once more. "Maybe I'm not supposed to know what I'll face. Maybe the real test is how I react in the moment."

The thought brought little comfort, but it was all he had. As the first rays of dawn began to creep through his window, Hinadori finally drifted into a fitful sleep.

It felt like mere moments later when a sharp knock jolted him awake. Yuki's stern voice came through the door. "Hinadori! It's time. Master Akio awaits at the Cave of Desolation."

Hinadori sat up, his body protesting the lack of rest. He dressed quickly, his mind still foggy with half-formed fears and unanswered questions.

As he stepped out into the cool morning air, Hinadori took a deep breath. He had no idea what awaited him in the Cave of Desolation, no clever strategies or secret preparations. All he had was himself, his experiences, and the strength he'd built over these past months.

"It will have to be enough," he murmured, squaring his shoulders as he made his way towards his next trial. Whatever shadows lurked in the depths of that cave, Hinadori was determined to face them head-on.

...

The mouth of the Cave of Desolation loomed before them, a yawning void that seemed to swallow the very light around it. Master Akio stood at its entrance, his scarred face illuminated by flickering torchlight, casting eerie shadows that danced across his stern features.

"Listen well," he growled, his voice low and menacing. "What awaits you inside is no mere test of skill or strength. The Cave of Desolation will strip away your defenses, lay bare your deepest fears, and force you to confront the darkest corners of your soul."

A chill ran down Hinadori's spine. He glanced at his fellow trainees, noting the tension in their postures. Daiki's jaw was clenched tight, a muscle twitching beneath his eye. Rin's usual calm demeanor had cracked, her fingers fidgeting with the hem of her sleeve. Even Hano, for all his bravado, looked uneasy, his massive frame seeming to shrink in on itself.

Akio continued, his voice dropping to a whisper that somehow carried more weight than a shout. "To succeed, you must overcome not just with physical prowess, but with the power of your mind and the strength of your spirit. Remember, not everything within is as it seems. Trust your instincts, but question your perceptions."

With those cryptic words hanging in the air, Akio gestured for them to enter. As they crossed the threshold, the cave mouth sealed behind them with a resounding boom, plunging them into darkness.

For a heart-stopping moment, there was nothing but the sound of their own ragged breathing. Then, slowly, an eerie phosphorescent glow began to emanate from the cave walls, casting everything in a sickly, otherworldly light.

The air grew thick and oppressive as they ventured deeper, each step echoing unnaturally in the stillness. Hinadori's mind raced with thoughts of Noke and his past in Tuchi Market.

Would he be forced to relive the pain of his parents' abandonment?

Or face the crushing weight of Omo's potential disappointment?

Rin's voice cut through the silence, barely above a whisper. "Statistically speaking, our greatest fears are likely to be rooted in past traumas or future uncertainties. If we approach this logically—"

"Oh, shut it," Daiki snapped, his usual arrogance tinged with fear. "Your precious logic won't save you here."

Hano shifted his massive frame in agreement, his massive fists clenching and unclenching rhythmically. "Yeah, I say we just punch our way through whatever comes at us."

Hinadori remained silent, observing the others. Their bickering was a thin veneer over their obvious fear, each trying to one-up the others to mask their own vulnerability.

Suddenly, the narrow passage opened into a vast cavern.

At its center stood an ancient stone monument, weathered and cracked with age. Four paths diverged from this point, each illuminated by a different colored flame that danced and flickered, casting long shadows across the cavern floor.

Carved into the monument were words that seemed to shimmer and shift as they approached:

"Four paths lie before you, each a mirror to the soul,

Choose wisely, for your deepest fears take their toll.

Red for passion, Blue for mind, Green for strength untamed,

Golden light for heart and spirit, where true worth is claimed."

Daiki, his impatience overriding caution, strode towards the path bathed in red light. "No time for riddles. Let's get this over with."

"Wait!" Rin called out, but Daiki had already disappeared down the crimson-lit tunnel.

Rin studied the monument intently, her analytical mind working overtime. "Fascinating. Each path seems to correspond to a specific aspect of our psyche. The blue path likely leads to fears related to intellect or failure of the mind."

With a deep breath, she squared her shoulders and chose the blue-lit path, disappearing into its cool glow.

Hano eyed the green-lit path, a gleam of challenge in his eyes. "Strength untamed, huh? Sounds like my kind of challenge."

He lumbered forward, the verdant light swallowing his massive frame.

Hinadori stood alone at the crossroads, the weight of choice heavy on his shoulders. He thought of Noke, of the mysterious dagger, of the greater purpose that seemed to be unfolding before him. The golden path called to him, its warm light somehow reminiscent of Omo's kind eyes.

Taking a deep breath, Hinadori stepped into the golden light.

The path narrowed as he walked, the walls seeming to close in around him. Just as claustrophobia began to set in, the passage opened into a scene that made his heart stop.

...

He stood in the middle of Tuchi Market, but it was wrong. The usually bustling streets were empty, an eerie silence hanging over the familiar stalls and alleyways. In the center of it all stood Omo, his weathered face etched with disappointment.

"Hinadori," Omo's voice echoed unnaturally. "You've forgotten us. Left us behind for your grand samurai dreams."

Hinadori felt his throat tighten. "No, Omo. I haven't forgotten. Everything I do is to become the samurai you saw in me. To honor your faith in me and forge myself into something greater than I was."

Omo's apparition shook his head sadly. "Pretty words from a pretty samurai. Look at you now, rubbing elbows with the elite. Wearing your fine silk training robes, that polished sword at your hip. So far from the boy in ragged clothes who used to beg for scraps. Your hands are too soft now, too clean of the dirt and grime of honest survival. You think you're better than us?"

The accusation stung, forcing Hinadori to confront the conflict he'd been avoiding. Was he betraying his roots in pursuit of a greater good? Or was this the only way to truly make a difference?

As he struggled with his response, the scene shifted. Suddenly, he was in the Bushido Academy, surrounded by his fellow trainees. They looked at him with disdain, whispering among themselves.

"Street rat," Daiki's voice carried over the others. "You'll never truly be one of us."

Rin's cool gaze cut through him. "Statistically speaking, someone of your background has a negligible chance of succeeding here."

Hano cracked his knuckles menacingly. "Why don't you go back to the gutters where you belong?"

Hinadori felt his resolve wavering, the weight of his two worlds threatening to crush him. Then, through the crowd, he saw a familiar face – Noke. She looked at him with a mixture of sadness and betrayal.

"You've forgotten who you are, Hinadori," she said softly. "You've lost your way."

It was this, more than anything, that steeled Hinadori's resolve. He straightened, looking each apparition in the eye.

"No," he said, his voice growing stronger with each word. "I haven't forgotten who I am or where I come from. But I refuse to be limited by it. I'm not choosing between worlds – I'm bridging them."

Suddenly, Akari's face appeared before him, her kind eyes now filled with accusation. 'You couldn't save me, Hinadori. You weren't strong enough then, and you're still not strong enough now. How many more will die because of your weakness?' The words cut deeper than any blade, reopening old wounds of guilt and failure.

He turned to them both and said. "I honor where I came from, and I'll never forget the lessons you taught me. but I can't fight the darkness that plagues our streets by remaining in the shadows. I must rise like a flame, burning away the corruption that keeps our people trapped in misery. Sometimes you have to climb above the storm to know where to strike the lightning."

To his fellow trainees, he said, "My background doesn't define me. It gives me strength, perspective, and a reason to fight. I've earned my place here, and I'll prove it every day."

Finally, he faced Noke. "I haven't lost my way. I'm forging a new path – one that honors our past and fights for our future. And I hope... I hope you'll be there with me when I do."

...

As he spoke, the apparitions began to fade, the market and academy dissolving around him. Hinadori found himself back at the stone monument, breathing heavily as if he'd run for miles.

The others were there too, each looking shaken in their own way. Daiki's usual arrogance had crumbled, revealing a vulnerability he quickly tried to mask. Rin's analytical calm was in tatters, her eyes wide with the realization that some fears couldn't be reasoned away. Hano's bravado had given way to a quiet thoughtfulness, his massive frame seeming smaller somehow.

They regarded each other warily, a newfound respect mingling with their lingering distrust. No one spoke of what they had seen, but the change in dynamics was palpable.

As they made their way back towards the entrance, the cave's otherworldly glow fading behind them, Hinadori felt the weight of his experience settling on his shoulders.

He had faced his fears, but the real challenge lay ahead – balancing his past with his future, his personal goals with the greater good.

The cave's exit loomed before them, a portal back to the world of sunlight and training. As they stepped through, each lost in their own thoughts, Hinadori caught a flicker of movement from the corner of his eye.

He turned, half-expecting to see another apparition. But there was nothing there – just the lingering echo of Omo's words and the knowledge that his journey was far from over.

As they emerged into the daylight, blinking against the sudden brightness, Master Akio stood waiting. His scarred face betrayed no emotion, but there was a glint in his eye that hadn't been there before.

"You have faced your fears," he said, his gravelly voice carrying across the training grounds. "But remember, confronting them once does not banish them forever. True strength lies in facing your fears every day, in every choice you make."

With those words hanging in the air, Akio turned and walked away, leaving the trainees to ponder the depths of what they had experienced.

Hinadori glanced at his fellow trainees. There was a new wariness in their eyes when they looked at him, tinged with a grudging respect. They had all been humbled by the cave, their carefully constructed personas cracked and revealing the vulnerabilities beneath.

As they made their way back to their quarters, Hinadori felt a renewed sense of purpose. The cave had forced him to confront the conflict between his past and his aspirations, but it had also shown him a path forward.

He would honor his roots while reaching for something greater.

And somewhere out there, Noke was facing her own trials.

Hinadori silently vowed to find her, to share what he had learned about the Shi no Ibuki and the forces at play. Whatever challenges lay ahead, he would face them with the strength of his past and the hope for their future.

The sun was setting as they reached the dormitories, casting long shadows across the training grounds. As Hinadori turned to enter his quarters, he caught a glimpse of movement from a high window in the council chambers.

For a split second, he thought he saw a familiar silhouette watching him.

But when he blinked, there was nothing there but the gathering darkness.

Shaking off the uneasy feeling, Hinadori entered his room.

Tomorrow would bring new challenges, new opportunities to prove himself. And with each trial, he would forge himself anew – a bridge between worlds, a force for change, and perhaps, someday, a true samurai.

Chapter 13: The Calm Before the Storm

Hinadori's eyes snapped open, his body tensing instinctively as he registered the unfamiliar silence. No shouts, no clanging of practice swords, no thunderous footsteps of trainees rushing to their morning drills. The quiet was... unsettling.

He rose cautiously, muscles aching from yesterday's trials in the Cave of Desolation. As he slid open the door to his quarters, he nearly collided with a figure standing just outside.

"Master Yumi!" Hinadori exclaimed, hastily bowing to hide his surprise.

The archery instructor stood before him, her usual serene expression tinged with an uncharacteristic urgency. "Come," she said simply, her voice low. "We must prepare you for what lies ahead."

Without waiting for a response, she turned and glided down the hallway. Hinadori hesitated for a moment, glancing back at his sparse room. Then, curiosity and a growing sense of anticipation propelling him forward, he followed.

They walked in silence, their footsteps echoing softly through the empty corridors. Hinadori's mind raced.

Why was Master Yumi here?

Where were the other trainees?

What new challenge awaited them?

Soon, they emerged into a secluded garden Hinadori had never seen before. The air was heavy with the sweet scent of cherry blossoms, their delicate petals drifting lazily on the morning breeze. A small stream wound its way through carefully arranged rocks, its gentle burbling a soothing counterpoint to the distant cries of birds welcoming the dawn.

Master Yumi gestured to a circle of smooth stones. "Sit," she instructed, lowering herself gracefully onto one of the rocks.

Hinadori complied, crossing his legs and feeling the cool, rough surface beneath him. He glanced around, expecting to see his fellow trainees, but they were alone.

"Close your eyes," Yumi said, her voice barely above a whisper. "Focus on your breath. Let the events of yesterday flow through you, neither clinging to them nor pushing them away."

Hinadori obeyed, allowing his eyelids to flutter shut. He concentrated on the steady rhythm of his own breathing, feeling the tension in his body slowly begin to ebb away.

As his mind stilled, memories of the Cave of Desolation surfaced. The fear, the doubt, the confrontations with his deepest insecurities – all of it washed over him like a wave. But instead of drowning in these emotions, Hinadori observed them with a newfound detachment.

His thoughts drifted to Omo, the old man's weathered face and kind eyes appearing in his mind's eye. A pang of loss shot through Hinadori's heart, but it was tempered now by gratitude for the lessons Omo had imparted.

Unbidden, Noke's face appeared next. Her mischievous grin, her fierce determination – attributes as familiar to Hinadori as his own reflection. His heart quickened at the thought of seeing her again, of sharing all he had learned about the Shi no Ibuki and the Wind of Death. She was the reason he pushed himself so hard, the driving force behind his determination to succeed in these trials.

"Breathe," Master Yumi's soft voice cut through his thoughts. "Return to the present moment. Feel the stone beneath you, the air in your lungs."

Hinadori took a deep breath, letting his swirling thoughts settle. As he exhaled, a new sense of clarity and purpose washed over him. Whatever the final trial might bring, he was ready to face it – not just for himself or for Noke, but for the greater purpose he was beginning to glimpse.

"Open your eyes," Master Yumi instructed.

As Hinadori's eyes fluttered open, he found Master Yumi studying him intently, her gaze piercing and unreadable.

"You carry a great weight, Hinadori," she said softly. "The burden of your past, the uncertainty of your future. But remember, a bow that is always strung will eventually break. You must learn to find balance – between tension and release, between your duty to others and your duty to yourself."

Hinadori nodded, absorbing her words. "Master Yumi," he ventured, "why are we here alone? Where are the others?"

A shadow passed over Yumi's face. "The final trial is not one you can face together. Each of you must walk your own path, confront your own demons. What awaits you... it will test not just your skills, but the very core of who you are and who you wish to become."

She rose gracefully to her feet, and Hinadori followed suit. "Come," she said, her voice taking on a note of finality. "It is time."

As they left the tranquil garden behind, Hinadori felt anticipation and dread settling in his stomach. Whatever lay ahead, he knew it would be unlike anything he had faced before. But as they walked, Hinadori found himself standing a little straighter, his steps a little more assured.

The sun had fully risen now, bathing the Bushido Academy in golden light. As they approached a section of the grounds Hinadori had never seen before, he caught sight of his fellow trainees in the distance. Daiki, Rin, and Hano stood apart from each other, their faces set in masks of determination tinged with apprehension.

Master Yumi stopped, turning to face Hinadori one last time. "Remember," she said, her voice low and intense, "true strength comes not from conquering others, but from mastering yourself. Trust in what you have learned, in who you are becoming. And above all, never forget why you fight."

With those words, she gestured for Hinadori to join the others.

Chapter 14: The Crucible of Unity

As Hinadori approached his fellow trainees, the air around them seemed to thicken with tension. Daiki, Rin, and Hano stood apart from each other, their faces masks of determination tinged with barely concealed apprehension. Master Ryugen and Master Toramaru stood before them, their presence commanding and austere.

Master Ryugen's golden eyes swept over the assembled trainees, his gaze seeming to pierce through their carefully constructed facades.

"You stand now at the threshold of your final trial," he intoned, his voice carrying the weight of ages. "What awaits you is not merely a test of skill or strength, but a crucible that will forge the very essence of your being."

Master Toramaru stepped forward, his massive frame casting a long shadow in the morning light. "This trial is known as The Crucible of Unity," he growled, his voice like gravel. "You will face challenges both individual and collective, testing not only your abilities but your capacity to work as a unit while maintaining your individual strengths."

Hinadori felt a chill run down his spine. He glanced at his fellow trainees, noting the subtle shifts in their postures. Daiki's jaw clenched tighter, a vein pulsing at his temple. Rin's fingers twitched, as if longing for a brush to calculate probabilities. Hano's massive fists clenched and unclenched rhythmically, his usual bravado subdued.

Master Ryugen continued, "You will enter a trance-like state, your consciousness transported to a realm shaped by your collective minds. There, you will find yourselves in different locations, each tailored to your unique personalities and mentalities."

"Your task," Master Toramaru interjected, "is to navigate this realm, completing challenges and helping its inhabitants. Only by working together, yet pushing each other to greater heights, will you succeed."

Hinadori's mind raced. He thought of Noke, of the mysterious dagger, of the greater purpose that seemed to be unfolding before him.

How would this trial bring him closer to understanding his role in it all?

The masters led them to a raised platform adorned with intricate symbols. As Hinadori stepped onto it, he felt a strange energy pulsing beneath his feet. He closed his eyes, taking a deep breath to center himself.

"Remember," Master Ryugen's voice seemed to come from far away, "what you experience will feel real. The dangers, the triumphs, the failures... all will leave their mark on your spirit. Choose wisely, act with purpose, and above all, never lose sight of who you are and why you fight."

A warm, enveloping light surrounded Hinadori.

He felt his consciousness slipping, drifting away from his physical body.

...

When he opened his eyes, he found himself standing in a bustling marketplace that bore an uncanny resemblance to Tuchi Market. Yet, everything was slightly off, as if viewed through a warped mirror.

Hinadori took in his surroundings, noting the subtle wrongness of it all. The colors were too vibrant, the sounds slightly muffled, the air carrying an otherworldly scent he couldn't quite place. As he began to walk, he realized he could see translucent images of his fellow trainees, each in their own distinct environment.

Daiki stood in what appeared to be a nobleman's court, his posture rigid and uncomfortable.

Rin found herself in a vast library, surrounded by scrolls and ancient tomes.

Hano was in some sort of gladiatorial arena, the roar of an unseen crowd echoing around him.

"Guys? *Guys?*"

Hinadori tried to call out to them, but his voice made no sound. He could see their lips moving, hear snatches of their words, but they seemed oblivious to his presence. A wave of frustration washed over him – he was witnessing their trials but powerless to help.

As he moved through the phantom marketplace, Hinadori became aware of the inhabitants. They were shimmering, half-formed figures that seemed to flicker in and out of existence. One of these apparitions approached him, an old woman with eyes that held an unnatural wisdom.

"Young warrior," she croaked, her voice echoing strangely, "our village suffers. The well has run dry, and without water, we will perish. Will you help us?"

Hinadori nodded, his throat tight. "I'll do what I can," he managed to say.

Daiki found himself surrounded by the suffocating grandeur of a noble's court, where gilt screens caught the lamplight and silk robes whispered against polished wooden floors. The assembled courtiers, their faces painted with practiced disdain, circled him like wolves sizing up wounded prey.

"But surely, young lord," one spectral courtier drawled, "you understand the delicate balance of power between the clans? Or has your esteemed lineage failed to prepare you for such... nuances?"

Daiki's face flushed, his voice wavering as he replied, "Of course I understand! It's just that... well, the situation is more complex than..."

Nearby, Rin faced an enormous, shimmering puzzle board that seemed to shift and change with each passing moment. Her brow furrowed in concentration as she muttered equations and theories under her breath.

"If I apply the theorem of... no, that's not right. Perhaps if I consider the variable of... argh!" She slammed her fist against the puzzle in frustration, a rare display of emotion from the usually composed strategist.

In a shadowy arena, Hano grappled with an opponent that seemed to match his every move. The muscular trainee's face was contorted with effort, veins bulging in his neck as he strained against his adversary.

"Why... won't... you... fall?!" Hano grunted, his usual boisterous confidence replaced by genuine struggle.

Hinadori longed to offer advice, to share the insights he'd gained from his time on the streets.

But he was merely an observer, forced to watch as they struggled and adapted.

As he searched for the well, Hinadori became aware of an unsettling presence. Out of the corner of his eye, he caught flashes of movement – a dark shape that seemed to flit just beyond his vision. When he turned to look, there was nothing there, but the feeling of being watched persisted.

The other trainees seemed unaware of this presence, focused entirely on their own challenges. Hinadori felt a chill run down his spine.

Was this part of the trial, or something else entirely?

He pressed on, trying to shake off the eerie feeling.

The well, when he found it, was a decrepit structure on the outskirts of the phantom village. As he approached, the darkness around him seemed to deepen, the air growing thick and oppressive.

The shadows around him began to dance and writhe, while whispers that seemed to come from nowhere and everywhere filled his ears. The very air shimmered with an unnatural purple light, and the temperature plummeted until his breath came out in frozen clouds.

"What-"

When he turned to look, there was nothing there, but the feeling of being watched persisted.

His training screamed at him to act, to warn the others, but something ancient and primal froze his tongue. This presence carried the weight of centuries of secrets better left buried.

A massive clawed hand burst from the shadows, seizing Hinadori by the throat. As those burning fingers tightened, the phantom marketplace shattered like glass around him, reality fracturing to reveal a void of swirling crimson and black. His feet dangled over nothingness as he was dragged into a realm beyond mortal understanding. He realized with a start that he had somehow slipped beyond the boundaries of the trial, into a realm that Master Yumi could no longer monitor or control.

In this strange new space, a creature materialized before him.

It stood nearly twice Hinadori's height, its muscular body a deep, angry red. Two massive horns protruded from its forehead, and its mouth was filled with sharp, fang-like teeth.

"An Oni," Hinasori breathed.

...

Indeed, the mystical creature's eyes gleamed with something ancient and malevolent, like pools of molten bronze that had witnessed a thousand years of mortal suffering. Its hands ended in wickedly curved claws.

The Oni wore nothing but a tiger-skin loincloth, and at its hip hung the Shi no Ibuki, its blade seeming to drink in what little light existed in this realm. The sight of the sacred dagger seemed to distort the very air around it, crackling with barely contained power.

"So," the Oni growled, its voice like rolling thunder, "you think you can save them, little samurai? You, who can't even save yourself?"

Hinadori's heart raced as he realized he was truly alone, facing a being of immense power and ancient knowledge. He steeled himself, trying to project a confidence he didn't feel. "I may not be able to save everyone, but I'll never stop trying."

The Oni's laughter shook the very fabric of this strange dimension. "Such noble words from one who knows nothing of his true self. Shall we peel back the layers of your past, Hinadori of Tuchi Market? Or should I say, Hinadori, son of the fleeing warrior and the woman who abandoned her child?"

Hinadori felt as if he'd been struck. "What... what are you talking about?"

The Oni's grin widened, revealing rows of razor-sharp teeth. "Your mother, boy. She left you not out of necessity, but desire. A different life called to her, one unburdened by a mewling infant."

Hinadori shook his head, trying to deny the Oni's words. "No, that's not possible. My mother loved me. She wouldn't—"

"Wouldn't she?" the Oni interrupted. "How well did you truly know her? The woman who bore you, then cast you aside like refuse?"

The Oni circled Hinadori, its massive form casting him in shadow. "And dear old Omo? Not the kind stranger you believed, but the blood of your blood.

Your mother's kin, tasked with watching over the child she cast aside. How does it feel, knowing your entire life has been built on lies?"

Hinadori staggered, his mind reeling from these profound truths. He wanted to deny them, to rage against the Oni's words, but deep down, he felt their ring of truth. "If what you say is true," he said, his voice trembling, "then why? Why would they do this?"

The Oni's eyes flashed with malicious glee. "Because you were never meant to exist, boy. You are a mistake, a burden, a reminder of their failures. Every kindness shown to you was born of guilt, not love."

Hinadori fell to his knees, overwhelmed by the weight of these revelations. The Oni loomed over him, its voice a mocking whisper. "Where is your determination now, little samurai? Where is your noble desire to save others when you can't even face the truth of your own existence?"

As Hinadori struggled to process this onslaught of revelations, something stirred within him. A memory of Noke's smile, of Omo's gentle guidance, of the bonds he'd formed at the academy.

These couldn't all be lies, could they?

In one fluid motion, Hinadori lunged forward, his hand closing around the Shi no Ibuki's hilt at the Oni's hip. The blade seemed to sing as he tore it free, resonating with something deep in his blood.

Hinadori looked up at the Oni, a new resolve burning in his eyes.

"You may know my past," he said, his voice growing stronger, "but you don't define my future. I am more than the sum of my parents' choices. I am Hinadori, and I choose my own path!"

The Oni's roar shook the very fabric of reality as it swung its massive kanabō. Hinadori barely managed to dodge, feeling the wind of its passage tear at his clothes. For what felt like hours, they danced a deadly ballet through the void - Hinadori's speed and training against the demon's raw power and centuries of combat experience. Blood flowed from countless wounds as the Shi no Ibuki clashed again and again with the Oni's weapons. Only when Hinadori embraced both his samurai training and his street-fighting instincts did he finally spot an opening, driving the sacred blade deep into the creature's core.

As the dimension began to fracture, Hinadori could barely stand. Blood flowed from a deep gash above his eye, and his left arm hung useless at his side. His outfit was shredded, revealing a tapestry of cuts and bruises across his torso.

The Oni's final words echoed in his mind: "You may have won this battle, boy, but the war for your soul has only just begun..."

As the last word left his lips, the Oni's club came crashing down... only to pass through Hinadori like smoke. The creature's form began to dissolve, its fearsome visage melting away into nothingness.

...

As the Oni vanished, the well behind it began to glow with a soft, pulsing light. Water bubbled up from its depths, clear and pure. The phantom villagers cheered, their joy palpable even in this strange, ethereal realm.

Hinadori turned, catching glimpses of his fellow trainees.

"Where have you been?" Daiki demanded. "We've all completed the trial, and you've been standing there like a statue!"

"Yeah," Hano chimed in, his voice gruff. "Why didn't you help us? Some teammate you turned out to be."

Rin studied Hinadori closely, her analytical mind clearly working overtime. "Your physical form remained, but your consciousness... it went somewhere else, didn't it?"

Suddenly, the world around them began to shimmer and fade.

Hinadori felt a pulling sensation, as if his consciousness was being drawn back to his physical body. As the phantom marketplace dissolved around him, he caught one last glimpse of a shadowy figure watching from a distance... a reminder that some challenges were yet to be faced.

...

Hinadori found himself back on the platform with his fellow trainees. They were looking at him with a mixture of confusion and suspicion.

Before Hinadori could respond to their earlier questions, he noticed Master Yumi approaching. Her usual serene expression was marred by a look of deep concern, her eyes fixed on the dagger still clutched in Hinadori's hand.

Without warning, Yumi reached out and snatched the dagger from Hinadori's grasp. Her eyes widened as she examined it, a mix of fear and recognition flashing across her face.

"How did you get THIS?" she demanded, her voice sharp and urgent.

Hinadori opened his mouth to explain, but the words caught in his throat. How could he possibly describe what had just happened?

The other trainees looked on in bewilderment, clearly sensing that something significant had occurred but unable to understand what.

Master Yumi's gaze swept over the group, her usual calm demeanor visibly shaken. "Class is dismissed," she announced abruptly. "Return to your quarters immediately. We will... discuss this another time."

As the trainees began to file away, casting confused and curious glances back at Hinadori and Master Yumi, Hinadori found himself rooted to the spot. He wanted to ask about the dagger, about the Oni, about everything he had learned. But the look in Yumi's eyes made it clear that now was not the time for questions.

"Hinadori," Yumi said quietly, her voice laced with an emotion he couldn't quite identify, "go with the others. And speak of this to no one. Do you understand?"

Hinadori nodded mutely, his mind reeling from both his encounter with the Oni and Yumi's unexpected reaction. As he turned to leave, he couldn't shake the feeling that he had stumbled upon something far larger and more complex than he could have imagined.

The dagger pulsed faintly in Yumi's hand, a reminder of the Oni's final words:

"The war for your soul has only just begun..."

Chapter 15: Whispers in the Shadows

"The dagger was secured, Saito. Explain." Yumi's voice was low and urgent.

The sun had long since set, casting the Bushido Academy in deep shadows. In a secluded chamber deep within the heart of the complex, flickering candlelight danced across the concerned faces of Master Yumi and Grand Master Saito. Between them on a low table lay the dagger, its blade still pulsing with an otherworldly energy.

Saito's brow furrowed as he examined the weapon. "It was. Or at least, it should have been. The fact that it appeared in his hands during the The Crucible of Unity trial is... troubling, to say the least."

"The timing of this...manifestation...is troubling," Yumi echoed, a rare note of frustration in her voice.

Saito nodded gravely. "An Oni spirit. And not just any Oni. One powerful enough to breach the barriers between realms."

Yumi paced the small room, her usual calm demeanor clearly shaken. "But why now? And why Hinadori? The boy is different, Saito."

"I've sensed it too," Saito admitted. "His connection to Noke, his mysterious past... there are too many coincidences for it to be mere chance."

They fell into a tense silence, the weight of unspoken fears hanging heavy in the air. Finally, Yumi spoke again, her voice barely above a whisper.

"The prophecies, then."

Saito's hand unconsciously moved to the hilt of his own sword - the legendary Wind of Death. "I pray it isn't so. But we must prepare for the worst."

"The students must be prepared."

Saito shook his head firmly. "No. They're not ready. The knowledge would only breed fear and uncertainty. We must continue their training as planned, push them harder than ever before."

"If war is truly on the horizon, they deserve to know what they're training for."

"They'll know soon enough," Saito replied, his voice heavy with the burden of command. "For now, let them focus on completing their samurai training. When the time comes, they'll need every skill we can teach them."

Yumi nodded reluctantly, her gaze drawn back to the dagger. "Hinadori will have questions.'

Saito's expression hardened. "Tell him nothing. Watch him closely, but reveal nothing of our suspicions. If he is indeed connected to these events as we fear, it's crucial that we understand the nature of that connection before taking any action."

"And if he presses the issue?" Yumi asked.

"Then we do what we must to protect the greater good," Saito said grimly. "Even if it means keeping secrets from those we've sworn to teach and protect."

The candlelight flickered, casting long shadows across the room. In that moment, both masters felt the weight of their responsibilities more keenly than ever before.

"Very well," Yumi said at last.

Saito nodded, a flicker of something – pride? concern? – passing across his face. "Do what you must, Yumi. Push them to their limits and beyond. The fate of our world may well rest on their shoulders, whether they know it or not."

As they prepared to leave the chamber, Saito paused, his hand on the door. "And Yumi? Be careful. If an Oni spirit is powerful enough to acquire that dagger through unknown means is indeed at work, none of us are safe. Trust no one completely – not even me."

Yumi's eyes widened at the implication, but she nodded her understanding. As they stepped out into the darkened hallway, the dagger safely secured once more, both masters couldn't shake the feeling that they were standing on the precipice of something far greater and more terrible than they had ever faced before.

In the shadows of the academy, unseen by either master, a pair of glowing eyes watched their departure. The air shimmered with malevolent energy, and for just a moment, the faint outline of massive horns could be seen before fading back into the darkness.

The coming storm was gathering strength, and the Bushido Academy... along with the rest of the world... was woefully unprepared for what lay ahead.

Chapter 16: The Forge of Adversity

The pre-dawn air was crisp and biting as Hinadori made his way to the training grounds. His mind raced with questions about the strange encounter with the Oni and Master Yumi's cryptic reaction to the dagger.

But today, he knew he had to focus.

The final combat trial loomed before them, the last hurdle before the tournament.

As he approached, he saw his fellow trainees already gathered. Tension hung in the air like a thick fog. Daiki paced restlessly, his usual swagger tempered by nervous energy. Rin stood perfectly still, her eyes closed in deep concentration. Hano cracked his knuckles, a predatory grin spreading across his face.

Master Akio's voice cut through the silence like a whip crack. "Gather around. Today, you prove your worth or expose your inadequacy."

The trainees formed a tight circle around him. Hinadori could feel their eyes on him, a mix of curiosity and disdain. He knew they still saw him as the outsider, the easy target.

Akio continued, his voice dripping with contempt. "You will face each other in combat. No holds barred. The last one standing earns a place in the tournament. The rest..." He paused, a cruel smile playing at his lips. "Well, let's just say you'd better not lose."

Murmurs rippled through the group. Hinadori's stomach clenched, but he kept his face impassive.

"First up," Akio barked, "Hano and Hinadori. Step into the circle."

Hano's grin widened as he shouldered his way past the others. "Finally," he growled, "a chance to put the street rat in his place."

Hinadori said nothing, simply taking his place across from Hano. He centered himself, remembering Yumi's lessons on focus and calm.

"Begin!" Akio's command rang out.

Hano charged forward like a raging bull, his massive fists swinging wildly. "What's wrong, gutter trash?" he taunted. "Too scared to fight back?"

Hinadori sidestepped, letting Hano's momentum carry him past. "Fighting isn't always about strength," he said softly, watching Hano's movements. "Sometimes it's about understanding."

Hano's massive fist caught Hinadori in the ribs, driving the air from his lungs. Stars exploded behind his eyes as he staggered backward, barely managing to stay on his feet. The bigger trainee pressed his advantage, each strike carrying enough force to shatter stone.

"Not so nimble now, are you?" Hano sneered, landing another devastating blow to Hinadori's shoulder.

Blood trickled from Hinadori's split lip as he narrowly avoided a punch that would have taken his head off. His body screamed in protest - ribs bruised, muscles burning. Every breath felt like swallowing fire. But in that pain, something clicked.

The river training, he realized. Don't fight the current - use it.

As Hano launched another powerful strike, Hinadori shifted his weight, remembering how he'd learned to move with the icy mountain waters rather than against them. Instead of trying to block the massive fist, he redirected it, letting Hano's own momentum carry him forward.

The bigger trainee stumbled, surprise flashing across his face. Before he could recover, Hinadori struck - not with power, but with precision. Quick jabs to pressure points, just as Master Akio had taught during those grueling isolation sessions.

Hano swung wildly, but his movements were slowing. Each time he committed to a powerful strike, Hinadori would flow around it, landing three smaller hits in return. Like water wearing down a mountain, gradually but inexorably.

"Stand... still!" Hano panted, frustration evident in his increasingly sloppy attacks.

Hinadori didn't respond, conserving his breath. His own body was a map of pain - bruises blooming across his torso, one eye swelling shut. But he could see Hano tiring, the bigger trainee's strength becoming his weakness as exhaustion set in.

The decisive moment came when Hano overextended on a desperate haymaker. Hinadori ducked under the swing and, in one fluid motion, swept Hano's legs while striking upward with his palm. The combination, born from countless hours of practice, sent the larger trainee crashing to the ground.

Hano tried to rise, his massive arms trembling with effort, but Hinadori had already moved into position, one hand poised to strike a vital point.

"Yield," Hinadori said quietly, his own voice rough with exhaustion.

Hano, refusing to do so, moved to attack again. But then he found himself on his knees, gasping for breath. Hinadori stood over him, calm and collected.

Akio's voice cut through the stunned silence. "Hinadori advances. Hano, get out of my sight."

As Hano limped away, Rin stepped forward, her eyes narrowed in calculation. "Don't get cocky," she said. "You only beat him because he beat himself."

Hinadori met her gaze steadily. "Ready when you are," he said quietly.

Their battle erupted like a storm. Rin moved like flowing water, each strike calculated to maximum efficiency. Her fist whistled past Hinadori's ear as he barely managed to dodge. He countered with a low sweep, but Rin had already anticipated it, leaping over his leg with practiced grace.

For what felt like hours, they traded blows in an intricate dance of violence. Blood trickled from a cut above Hinadori's eye, while Rin's breath came in ragged gasps.

Neither would yield.

The tide turned when Hinadori began incorporating unpredictable moves from his street fighting days. A feint turned into an elbow strike. A defensive roll became an opportunity for a surprise counter. Rin's perfect form began to crack against his unconventional style.

"Fight properly!" she demanded, frustration breaking her usual calm as another wild strike slipped through her guard.

"This is proper," Hinadori responded, ducking under her perfectly executed kick. "It's just not what you expect."

The end came suddenly.

Rin's precision finally betrayed her as Hinadori baited her into overcommitting to a strike. He slipped inside her guard, swept her leg, and in one fluid motion pinned her arm behind her back."

"Hinadori advances," Akio announced, a note of surprise in his voice. "Rin, you disappoint me."

Daiki stepped into the circle, his eyes blazing with determination. "Looks like it's just you and me, street rat," he sneered. "Time to show you what real skill looks like."

Hinadori's body already bore the marks of his previous battles. His right eye was beginning to swell, his ribs ached from Hano's powerful strikes, and fresh bruises were blooming across his torso. Blood from his split lip had dried on his chin.

But there was no time to rest, even when he felt a flicker of apprehension. Daiki was the most well-rounded fighter, combining Hano's strength with Rin's technique. So he pushed the feeling aside, focusing on the present moment.

The fight was brutal from the start. Daiki pressed his advantage, forcing Hinadori onto the defensive. His strikes came fast and hard, each one calculated to wear Hinadori down.

But Hinadori had learned more than just fighting techniques during his time at the academy. He had learned patience, endurance, and most importantly, how to read his opponents.

As the battle raged on, Hinadori began to see patterns in Daiki's attacks. He started to anticipate, to counter more effectively. Frustration began to show on Daiki's face.

Suddenly, Daiki's stance shifted.

Hinadori's eyes widened as he recognized the setup for the forbidden technique, the very move that had caused so much trouble before.

Time seemed to slow.

Hinadori saw the strike coming, saw the raw power behind it. But instead of trying to block or dodge, he moved with it, redirecting Daiki's force away from both of them.

Daiki stumbled, thrown off balance by the unexpected maneuver. In that moment of vulnerability, Hinadori struck. A series of quick, precise hits, and Daiki was on the ground, the wind knocked out of him.

The training ground fell silent.

"The preliminary matches have concluded," Akio announced. "Now our top students will determine the Academy's champion."

The four remaining trainees - Hinadori, Daiki, Rin, and Hano - formed a square at the center of the training ground. Each had proven their worth through grueling elimination matches. Now they would face each other in turn.

Rin and Hano clashed first. Her precise strikes eventually overcame his raw power, though both showed skills worthy of the tournament. Daiki faced Hinadori in a match that had the entire academy holding its breath. Their styles contrasted sharply - Daiki's perfect form against Hinadori's adaptive technique. Though Hinadori emerged victorious, Daiki's performance left no doubt about his qualification.

The final matches saw each student face their remaining opponents. Hano's victory over Daiki was decisive, his powerful strikes finally finding their mark. Rin and Hinadori's battle became an instant legend in the academy - a perfect blend of technique and improvisation that ended with Hinadori's narrow victory.

When the dust settled, all four had proven themselves tournament-worthy, but Hinadori's undefeated record made him the clear champion.

"The Academy has chosen its representatives," Akio declared. "These four will carry our honor to the tournament. Hinadori, you have earned the right to lead them."

Hinadori stepped back, his breathing controlled despite the exertion. With precise movements, he bowed formally to his fallen opponent before turning to return to his position, leaving Daiki to rise on his own.

Kneeling formally before Master Akio, he placed his training sword on the ground before him and bowed deeply, forehead nearly touching the earth in a show of complete respect.

Akio's voice cut through the moment. "The match is concluded. Hinadori has proven himself worthy. You four have earned your places in the tournament. Leave now and prepare yourselves. The real challenge awaits."

As the other trainees filed away, Hinadori turned to find all four masters regarding him - Kaito's stern approval, Akio's measured assessment, Toramaru's grudging respect, and Yumi's quiet acknowledgment. Each had contributed to forging him into what he had become.

Hinadori moved into a deep bow. Each master in turn bowed slightly - a rare gesture of respect that spoke volumes. No words were needed; he had earned his place among them.

Chapter 17: What's To Come

A soft mew pierced the pre-dawn stillness, jolting Hinadori from his fitful sleep.

He blinked, disoriented, as his eyes fell upon a familiar orange and white form perched on his windowsill.

The kitten from that fateful night... the night he had overheard the masters' secret conversation... stared at him with unblinking golden eyes.

"How did you get in here?" Hinadori murmured, reaching out to stroke the kitten's fur.

As his fingers made contact, a jolt of energy coursed through him.

Visions flashed before his eyes... the Oni's terrifying visage, the glowing dagger, Master Yumi's concerned face. The kitten leapt from the windowsill and darted out the door, leaving Hinadori gasping and confused.

Shaking off the strange encounter, Hinadori dressed quickly.

As he stepped into the hallway, he noticed an unusual buzz of activity. Trainees hurried past, whispering excitedly among themselves. Catching snippets of conversation, Hinadori pieced together that Grand Master Saito had called for an assembly, something unprecedented in the academy's recent history.

Following the flow of students, Hinadori found himself in the grand courtyard. Mist clung to the ground, giving the gathering an unearthly atmosphere. At the center stood Grand Master Saito, his imposing figure amplified by the reverent silence that fell as he raised his hand.

"Trainees of the Bushido Academy," Saito's voice rang out, clear and commanding. "You stand here today not as students, but as warriors. Each of you has been tested, pushed to your limits, and forged in the fires of adversity."

Hinadori felt a swell of pride, remembering the trials he had overcome. He noticed Daiki, Rin, and Hano nearby, their faces a mix of anticipation and nervousness.

Saito continued, his eyes sweeping over the assembled trainees. "The time has come to reveal the true purpose of your training. For generations, our academy has stood as a bulwark against the forces that would threaten the balance of our world. And now, a great challenge looms before us."

A murmur rippled through the others. Hinadori leaned forward, his heart racing.

"The Shugendo Temple," Saito's voice took on a grave tone, "our ancient rivals and counterparts, have grown powerful. Too powerful. Their practices threaten to upset the delicate equilibrium that keeps our realm safe from darker forces."

Hinadori's mind reeled. The Shugendo Temple... where Noke had gone.

"In one month's time," Saito declared, "we will face the Shugendo Temple in ritual combat. This is not merely a test of skill, but a battle for the very soul of our world. The victors will gain the right to shape the future of our magical arts."

As Saito spoke, the mist in the courtyard began to swirl and take shape. Ghostly figures appeared – samurai and monks locked in eternal combat. The trainees gasped, some stumbling back in shock.

"Behold," Saito's voice thundered, "the echoes of battles past. Our ancestors have fought this war for centuries, each generation taking up the mantle. And now, it falls to you."

The spectral warriors faded, leaving the courtyard in an eerie silence. Saito's gaze seemed to linger on Hinadori for a moment before sweeping across the assembled trainees.

"Some of you have shown exceptional promise," he said, a hint of pride in his voice. "You will lead the charge against the Shugendo Temple. But make no mistake – every one of you has a crucial role to play."

Hinadori felt the weight of expectation settle on his shoulders. He glanced at his fellow trainees, seeing a mix of determination and fear on their faces.

Saito raised his arms, his voice rising to a crescendo. "From this day forward, you enter a new phase of your training. You have earned the right to represent our academy, to walk the path of accelerated training under my direct guidance. Make no mistake - you are still students, but students who have proven worthy of greater challenges."

As Saito's words rang out, a strange wind swept through the courtyard. Cherry blossoms swirled around the trainees, their delicate petals a stark contrast to the gravity of the moment. Hinadori caught one in his hand, marveling at its perfection before it dissolved into mist.

Whatever revelations awaited, whatever challenges loomed on the horizon, Hinadori knew that his journey was far from over.

In fact, it felt like it was only just beginning.

Chapter 18: The Eve of Destiny

One Month Later

The Bushido Academy buzzed with an energy unlike anything Hinadori had experienced before. Trainees rushed back and forth, packing supplies and checking weapons. The air was thick with a mixture of excitement, nervousness, and determination.

Hinadori stood in his sparse room, carefully folding his few possessions into a small pack. His hand lingered on the worn fabric of the shirt Omo had given him, a reminder of where he'd come from and how far he'd come.

A knock at the door interrupted his reverie.

"Enter," he called out.

A sharp rap at his door announced Yuki's presence.

"Hinadori! The others are assembled and waiting."

As he opened the door, he was surprised to find not just Yuki, but also Daiki leaning against the opposite wall.

"Hurry up, street rat," Daiki said, though the old insult carried a hint of grudging respect. "We've got a long journey ahead. Almost ready?"

Hinadori nodded. "Just about. You?"

Daiki shrugged, trying to appear nonchalant. "Born ready. These Shugendo monks won't know what hit them."

"Don't underestimate them," Hinadori warned. "Remember what Master Kaito taught us about measuring our opponents."

Daiki's face softened slightly. "Yeah, yeah. Speaking of which, we should probably go say our goodbyes to the instructors. You coming?"

Hinadori nodded, shouldering his pack. As they left the room, they were joined by Rin and Hano in the hallway.

At first, the four of them walked in silence, each lost in their own thoughts.

Then Rin spoke first. "I've calculated our optimal route to the Shugendo Temple. If we maintain a steady pace, we should arrive with ample time to prepare for the ritual combat."

Hano grinned, cracking his knuckles. "All this planning is well and good, but I say we just charge in and show them what real warriors can do!"

The group made their way to the main courtyard, where the instructors had gathered to bid farewell to their students. Master Kaito stood rigid, his scarred face as stern as ever. Master Akio's eyes gleamed with a fierce pride, while Master Yumi's serene expression belied the concern in her eyes.

Grand Master Saito stepped forward as the trainees assembled. "You stand before us not as students, but as warriors of the Bushido Academy. Each of you carries with you not just the skills we've taught, but the spirit of generations who have fought to maintain balance in our world."

His eyes swept over the gathered trainees, lingering for a moment on Hinadori. "Remember your training, trust in each other, and above all, uphold the honor of our academy. May your blades be swift and your spirits unbreakable. Remember that the masters will follow in their own time, traveling separately to maintain the ancient traditions of the competition. Each school will arrive with their own procession of leaders and sacred artifacts."

As the trainees began to file out, Hinadori approached Master Yumi. She smiled softly, placing a hand on his shoulder.

"Hinadori," she said, her voice low. "Look at you—a far cry from that lost boy who stumbled through our gates. But don't forget, true strength isn't born of skill alone. It's in the bonds you choose to forge, the loyalty you earn. Without that, all the power in the world is nothing."

Hinadori nodded, feeling a lump form in his throat. "Thank you, Master Yumi. For everything."

Next, he faced Master Akio, who regarded him with a fierce intensity. "Boy," Akio's scarred face twisted into a fierce snarl. ' '"You've survived my training - barely. But survival isn't victory. Show them what it means to face a warrior of the Bushido Academy."

Hinadori gave a sharp nod and said nothing more.

Master Kaito was last, his face an impassive mask. "Hinadori," he said simply. "Remember, the sword is an extension of your will. Wield it with purpose and clarity."

As Hinadori turned to leave, Kaito's hand shot out, gripping his arm. Remember your forms," Kaito said flatly. "Perfect execution. Nothing less."

Hinadori rejoined his companions, each of them having said their own good-byes. As they approached the academy gates, Grand Master Saito appeared before them one last time.

"Hinadori," he said, his voice carrying a weight of unspoken meaning. "Come, boy. I must speak with you."

The others looked on curiously as Hinadori stepped aside with Saito.

"The cherry blossoms bloom even in winter, Hinadori. Remember that when the shadows lengthen." His voice carried the weight of steel, each word precise and loaded with hidden meaning.

Hinadori held his tongue as he processed Saito's words.

Saito's eyes blazed with intensity. "When steel meets shadow, truth reveals itself. Be ready for that moment, Hinadori. The ancestors watch."

Before Hinadori could ask any more questions, Saito stepped back, raising his voice. "Go now, and may the spirits of our ancestors guide your blades!"

As Hinadori rejoined his companions, Daiki raised an eyebrow. "What's wrong, street rat?" Daiki sneered, though there was a hint of envy in his voice. "Master's pet getting special instructions?"

"Nothing," Hinadori lied, his mind racing.

The group set out, the gates of the Bushido Academy closing behind them with a resounding boom. As they crested the first hill, Hinadori paused, looking back at the place that had become his home.

Rin noticed his hesitation. "Calculating the probability of regret?" she asked, her voice sharp with practiced precision. "I'd estimate about a 67% chance you're reconsidering your life choices."

Hinadori shook his head. "No, just... taking it all in. Everything's about to change, isn't it?"

Hano clapped him on the back, nearly knocking him over. "That's the spirit, street rat! Adventure awaits!"

As they continued their journey, the Bushido Academy fading into the distance behind them, Hinadori couldn't shake the feeling that they were walking into something far bigger and more dangerous than any of them realized. The weight of Saito's secret message sat heavy in his mind.

But as he looked at his companions – Daiki's determined stride, Rin's calculating gaze, Hano's boundless enthusiasm – he felt a surge of confidence. Whatever challenges they faced in the coming days, they would face them together.

The road stretched out before them, winding through forests and mountains towards the distant Shugendo Temple. With each step, Hinadori felt himself moving further from the street rat he once was and closer to the warrior he was becoming.

As the sun began to set on their first day of travel, casting long shadows across the path, Hinadori silently renewed his vow. He would uncover the truth behind this conflict, protect his friends, and somehow, someway, find a path to peace that honored both the Bushido Academy and the Shugendo Temple.

The journey had only just begun, but already, Hinadori could feel the winds of destiny howling for blood.

Chapter 19: The Road to Fate

A *Few Days Later*

The sun hung low on the horizon, painting the sky in vibrant hues of orange and pink as Hinadori and his companions made camp for the night.

They had been traveling for three days, the Bushido Academy now a distant memory behind them.

As Hano struggled to start a fire, Rin methodically laid out their supplies, her brow furrowed in concentration. Daiki paced the perimeter of their camp, his hand never far from the hilt of his sword.

"You know," Hano grunted, striking flint against steel for the umpteenth time, "I'm starting to think our journey is cursed. Can't even get a simple fire going."

Rin rolled her eyes. "Or perhaps your technique is simply flawed. Here, allow me."

She knelt beside Hano, arranging the kindling more efficiently before striking the flint. Sparks flew, and within moments, a small flame flickered to life.

Daiki snorted. "Well, well. Looks like the bookworm has some practical skills after all."

Rin's eyes narrowed. "Unlike some, I believe in being prepared for all eventualities."

"Oh yeah?" Daiki challenged. "Then tell me, oh wise one, what's your plan for when we actually face these monks? Going to bore them to death with statistics?"

As Rin and Daiki's argument escalated, with Hano eagerly jumping in, Hinadori slipped away from camp. He needed space to clear his head. He calmly walked away and leaned against a nearby tree. He closed his eyes, but he could still hear the others arguing.

Hano let out a booming laugh. "Meditation? Now? I'd rather wrestle a bear. I don't need meditation to prepare," Hano growled, pacing the campsite. "Just point me at the enemy."

Rin's laugh was cold as winter frost. "Of course you don't. Your statistical probability of thinking before acting is approximately zero."

"At least I can fight without having to calculate the angle of my punches," Hano shot back.

Daiki sneered, polishing his blade with practiced precision. "You're both embarrassing to the Academy. A brute and a bookworm."

As their argument escalated, Hinadori slipped to the ground and leaned against the tree trunk. settling into the meditation pose Master Yumi had taught him. The sounds of his companions' bickering faded as he centered himself.

...

Suddenly, the air grew thick with incense. A familiar presence washed over him.

"Troubled, my boy?"

Hinadori's eyes snapped open. There, sitting across from him, was Omo - not as he'd last seen him, broken and dying, but strong and vital.

"This isn't possible," Hinadori whispered.

Omo's weathered face creased in a smile. "Many impossible things become possible when destiny calls." His expression grew serious. "The tournament grounds await, Hinadori. But the true battle won't be fought with swords and fists."

"What do you mean?"

"Light and shadow dance eternally," Omo said, his form beginning to fade. "Remember who you are, what the streets taught you. Sometimes the greatest victory comes from refusing to fight at all."

...

As Omo's spirit dissipated like morning mist, Hinadori felt a new clarity settling over him. Slowly, he returned from his meditation and he found his companions' anger had mellowed into reminiscence. He sat quietly in the shadows, listening as they spoke of the lives they'd left behind.

As the night deepened, their conversation drifted to lighter topics. Hano regaled them with outrageous tales from his hometown, while Rin surprised everyone with her dry, deadpan humor. Even Daiki let his guard down, sharing stories of his childhood pranks.

As the fire died down, they drew lots for watch duty. Hinadori pulled the shortest stick.

"First watch it is," he said, settling into position as the others prepared for sleep.

As his companions drifted off to sleep, Hinadori took first watch. He stared into the dying embers of the fire, feeling the weight of secrets crushed against his chest, each breath a battle against the crushing responsibility. One more burden and he felt he might crack the earth beneath him.

Suddenly, a rustle in the nearby bushes caught his attention. Hinadori's hand went to his sword, muscles tensing. But instead of an enemy, out stepped the familiar orange and white kitten from the academy.

"You again?" Hinadori whispered, incredulous. "How did you follow us all this way?"

The kitten merely mewed softly, padding over to curl up in Hinadori's lap. As he absentmindedly stroked its fur, Hinadori felt a strange sense of calm wash over him. Whatever mysteries lay ahead, whatever challenges they would face, he knew they would face them together.

The kitten purred contentedly, and Hinadori smiled. In that moment, as the kitten's eyes met his, Hinadori saw something ancient and knowing in their depths. A flash of understanding struck him like lightning... sometimes the greatest powers hide in plain sight, waiting for the right moment to reveal their true nature.

Chapter 20: The Opening Gates

Three Days Before the Tournament

As the sun crested the horizon, bathing the world in a soft golden glow, Hinadori and his companions crested the final hill. Before them, nestled in a lush valley surrounded by mist-shrouded mountains, stood the Shugendo Temple.

The sight took their breath away.

Unlike the stark, militant architecture of the Bushido Academy, the Shugendo Temple was a marvel of organic design. Its sweeping roofs and graceful spires seemed to grow from the very mountainside, adorned with intricate carvings and vibrant murals.

"Well," Daiki breathed, breaking the awed silence, "it's certainly... different."

Rin's eyes darted over the structure, analyzing every detail. "The defensive capabilities are impressive, despite its aesthetic appeal. Look at how the terraces are arranged - perfect for archers."

Hano cracked his knuckles, a grin spreading across his face. "Pretty or not, we're here to show them what real warriors can do."

Hinadori remained silent, his mind racing. Somewhere within those walls was Noke. And somewhere, a monk named Takeshi who might hold the key to unraveling the mysteries that had plagued him since leaving the academy.

As the sun crested the horizon, bathing the world in soft golden light, Hinadori and his companions emerged from the forest path. Before them stretched the ancient tournament grounds - a vast clearing nestled between three mountain peaks.

Unlike the stark architecture of the Bushido Academy, this place radiated raw, primal power. Stone markers, worn smooth by centuries of wind and rain, formed a perfect circle. Within, the ground had been meticulously maintained, but no grass grew - as if the earth itself knew blood would soon be spilled here.

They approached the gates in silence, their faces set in masks of determination. Some moments required no words.

As they approached the ornately carved gates with scenes of spiritual enlightenment and magical feats, Hinadori felt a strange energy in the air. It was as if the very stones of the temple were alive with an ancient power.

The others nodded, straightening their postures and setting their faces in masks of determination.

Just as they reached the foot of the steps leading to the gate, a low, resonant tone filled the air.

The massive doors began to swing open.

www.ingramcontent.com/pod-product-compliance
Lightning Source LLC
Chambersburg PA
CBHW030903200726
48289CB00003B/881